Finding Joy after Sorrow

The Collected Works of Beth Carol Solomon

Beth Carol Solomon

FriesenPress

One Printers Way
Altona, MB R0G 0B0
Canada

www.friesenpress.com

First Edition — 2022

Revised edition of Collected Works (published in 2002)

ISBN
978-1-03-915259-5 (Hardcover)
978-1-03-915258-8 (Paperback)
978-1-03-915260-1 (eBook)

1. FICTION, SHORT STORIES (SINGLE AUTHOR)

Distributed to the trade by The Ingram Book Company

I dedicate this writing in loving memory to my Mom and Dad who have always been supportive and encouraging and inspired me to achieve my goals and who taught me what unconditional love and family are all about.

To Doctor Samuel Silber and Doctor Irwin Blatt, whose patience and aid through rough times gave me the confidence to believe in myself to succeed in my endeavors. I would also like to thank my friend, Blanche Ciccone, who has helped me tremendously with the editing of this script. I am grateful for her assistance and support.

PART ONE:

NON-FICTION STORIES OF SPECIAL PEOPLE AND EVENTS IN MY LIFE

PART TWO:

TWO NOVELLAS

THESE THREE

ARLENE AND RUBIN: A LOVE STORY

PART ONE

ARLENE

PART TWO

RUBIN

PART THREE

ARLENE AND RUBIN
THE BEGINNING

PART FOUR

ARLENE AND RUBIN
LATER

INTRODUCTION

This revision of my previously published book, Collected Works, now retitled Finding Joy After Sorrow: The Collected Works by Beth Carol Solomon, is composed in two segments. The first is non-fiction. The second consists of two fictional accounts of children with special needs who were abused and bullied. Also at the end of this writing are resources that I highly recommend to anyone who has suffered from abuse, bullying, violence, or those dealing with special needs.

The first part consists of people and events that have shaped me to be confident, to be a person of value, to believe in myself, to achieve greatness in my future endeavors, to forgive and understand myself and others who caused me injustices, to see problems and challenges as opportunities to learn and grow, to be positive and optimistic, to put troubling, compromising situations into proper perspective, to learn to settle differences without anger, and to view life as a wonderful adventure which depends on one's attitude.

The second part contains two novellas entitled 'These Three' and 'Arlene and Rubin: A Love Story.'

'These Three' depicts a compassionate, loving special education teacher/psychologist who herself suffered personal heartaches. She helps three children with special needs to love, forgive, care, and achieve.

'Arlene and Rubin: A Love Story' introduces two sexually abused adolescents who struggled with inner turmoil but with support and love, they learn to care for each other, as well as to cope and come to terms with the challenges they faced to have a better future.

PART ONE:

NON-FICTION STORIES OF SPECIAL PEOPLE AND EVENTS IN MY LIFE

THE CANDY LADY

She had the name of an empress—Napoleon's wife. Her name was Josephine. People called her Josie, not I. I called her Jo—Lady Jo—The Candy Lady, my lady friend from the Arlene Street bus.

I had seen her many times waiting for the bus with the others. I didn't know her. She had thick blonde hair and dressed refined in black; a warm, maternal lady.

I wanted to know her. She sat in front of me on the bus. While others spurned me with scorn for my problems and episodes, she didn't. She reached out—literally and figuratively. She reached into her pocketbook and handed me a piece of candy. Either that or a tissue. I leaned over and told her a lamentation. She was a good listener. Always attentive toward me. Never judging or condemning me. She sat near me, squeezed my hand and told me gleefully how cute I was. I told her about my uncle dying of cancer. She was the first and only person on the bus I told. And I didn't even know her last name. She told me about herself. We listened to each other with interest. She held my hand on the bus so I wouldn't fall. She held my books for me once when I didn't have a seat on the bus. Every time I saw her, she smiled, her small dark eyes sparkling. Once, she brushed her hand against my cheek, and said "I love you, honey." I was enthralled. She told me that another time in the beauty parlor, where she blew me a kiss while she told me I put on weight. I went on a diet at once.

She was not exceedingly verbal, but that was fine. She was quiet, sensitive, and loving. She let me in her home once, and I was in heaven. She was quite elderly but had all her faculties—including warmth and understanding. Never an unkind word out of her mouth. "Don't make a scene," she said, concerned as she reached out to me. I didn't after that.

I didn't know her at first, this handsomely dressed lady with thick blonde hair, tiny brown eyes like opals, and perfectly manicured nails and soft hands. I was glad we knew each other. Thank you, Jo. Thank you for you.

Note: Josephine died in 2006 from natural causes. Rest in peace, dear Jo. I love you forever and ever a day and always. I will never forget you. You will always be in my heart.

EDNA: PORTRAIT OF AN OUTSTANDING SENIOR CITIZEN

I look at her picture, a photograph I took of her over thirty-three years ago in the summer when I met her on a Canadian Panoramic Domenico Bus Tour, an elderly lady who became my friend. Edna was her name, short and blonde with hazel eyes, just an ordinary looking senior citizen who loved children, the elderly, the frail, the sick, plants, and animals. She loved and was loved.

She died. I knew it was just a matter of time until she would depart from this world. Edna had leukemia and was three quarters of a century old, but she never complained, even about her critical and cold mother. She exerted herself for others, including me.

When I'd call her with a problem, she would listen to my stories of cruelties by others. She was sympathetic and never condemned or judged me harshly. When I was upset, her gentle voice made me feel better.

I often told her how wonderful and beautiful she was. Though she was ill and tired at times, she was always on top of things. Edna was nominated for the Senior Citizen Woman of the Year award in 1988 for her volunteer work in a nursing home, comforting a blind/deaf old lady who had no one to love. She directed a nursery school for twenty years after teaching pre-school children.

Edna loved watching God's living things bloom. She took care of her garden and planted seeds for herbs, plants, flowers, fruits, and vegetables, watching them blossom.

Edna had a dog of fifteen years named Heidi, who, when she became ill, Edna had no choice but to put her to sleep, which naturally broke her heart. Edna never let her dog out of her sight. She would be out walking the dog before dawn and late at night, when all were dead to the world. The dog stayed by her side and followed her wherever she went.

Every time I telephoned her, she was sprite and happy, always doing something that day, either at her church, Sunday School, at her garden or herb clubs, tending to her garden, talking to her friends, or being with her children and grandchildren.

On the third Saturday of July, she had diarrhea, still we told each other we loved each other and blew kisses as always. She was an affectionate, loving person. However, when I called her the next day, she seemed weary and tired and said she slept all day for she was not feeling well but stated that we would talk again. I do not remember the "I love you" and kiss. It all took but a second, but I thought nothing of it at the time. We never spoke after that day. Edna died three days later in the hospital.

I found out about Edna's demise the following Saturday when I turned for a second toward the couch in the den and saw Edna's name in big, bold letters in the newspaper. Edna was dead. My heart stopped. I did not want to believe it. Why did she have to die? She really was not that old. And she was a good, kind, and wonderful woman though I knew she was sick. I cried, wanting to die too for I wanted to be with her. I never had the opportunity to say good-bye to her.

I sent a contribution to her church and a sympathy card to her children, with a letter containing loving thoughts about their mother.

Edna is free now and at peace, where she is no longer in pain, for she is in God's loving hands. She has performed her mission in life by helping, serving, and loving others unselfishly. It was her time to leave earth, to go on to another dimension where there is no suffering, and no one gets sick. Her spirit lives on forever even after her physical demise.

I authored a poem for her seventy-fifth birthday in April and sent her a gardening book attached with a friendship card and letter. At least she died knowing I loved her, and she me. For this, I am grateful to have known her. Edna will always play an important part in my life, and I will never forget her.

True, I wanted to be with Edna, but it was not my time. That is up to God, for He knows best. Then I reasoned, Edna would want me to be happy and go on living, not be sad, shed tears, or be miserable in any way. I will live and love like Edna did, for Edna.

DOROTHY: MY LOVELY LADY FRIEND FROM THE BUS

She was just another passenger on my morning bus. I did not want to know her. I did not know why, but I did and was glad. She did not look like anyone special. She was just an ordinary, elderly lady with disheveled blonde hair and blue-green eyes.

Her name was Dorothy. She was going through a divorce from her second husband, a philanderer, in addition to problems she was having with her divorced, middle-aged daughter who was living with her.

I met her in August 1987 when I noticed she was working on college registration forms. I thought to myself, 'this lady is in college.' How wonderful, being I was a professional student. Therefore, I was interested, and I asked her what courses she was taking. I informed her I was academically oriented. We hit it off.

She told me she worked in the medical building in the college where she took classes. Her job as a Departmental Secretary required her to deal with sick people and their families. Dorothy told me about the wife of a heart patient. We discussed a movie, which dealt with Alzheimer's disease. I told her I was helping with the cause and that I was also involved with senior citizens, and she informed me of places I might consider.

I told her about my personal life, which she commented and supported me on. She also shared her life with me. She set an example of forgiveness and understanding when she told me about a sister who used to make trouble for her and her other siblings, and that their mother preferred her. Dorothy told me once that her mother had all the siblings meet and explained that she felt this sister was weak and that was why she had been especially partial to her when they were growing up. Though Dorothy did not agree with her mother, she understood, for she said, "In my mother's mind, she was right." She told me she loved her sister despite her 'weakness' and was closer to this sister than to any of her other siblings. This made Dorothy special, for I wished I could be that forgiving.

We met for lunch when we were able, and she always told me stories as she did when we rode on the bus. She knew I had weaknesses and accepted them, like one time when I was upset in the street. She comforted me. She put her hand under my chin gently. She was not embarrassed to be with me. She mentioned I had a good personality, which I felt was nice, being she knew about my difficulties.

Dorothy was a stranger to me at one time, but I was very glad she became my friend for she was very special to me.

Rest in peace, Dorothy. I love you forever and a day.

THE 'REPLACEMENT'

Dorothy Phillips, my ninth-grade English teacher, was a tall, thin, ungainly, weak, and sickly woman who could barely stand up straight, or walk right, and required a cane and special chair. Her hair was short, dark, and wavy. Her eyes were framed with thick, black-rimmed glasses. Her face was tired, saggy, and wrinkled.

At first, I resented and refused to like and accept her, because she replaced another teacher I loved the previous semester who, in turn, said Mrs. Phillips—who knew me briefly—requested that I would be with her in English class again. I did not want her to love me and prayed she would die. Also, I'd show up late for work or keep her waiting without an explanation. I actually looked for reasons to hate her, which was hard, but there were three incidents that seemed to underscore and validate my feelings. One time, she sided with two girls who annoyed me on the bus. Another incident took place in the cafeteria, where she said I threw things, when all I did was hurl a potato chip bag across the room and act up. She graded a word wrong on my English midterm that I knew was correct, but she thought I changed my answer because at other times I did that. I dwelled on these three episodes continually, but Mrs. Phillips sided with me more times than not when the other children teased me, by asking for their names, writing them down, sending for, scolding, reprimanding, and punishing them by calling their parents. When anyone called me 'stupid' or 'psycho' or 'crazy,' she'd stick up for me and become indignant by saying, "Who are you calling stupid? You should receive her marks!" From time to time, Mrs. Phillips called me into her office, concerned about my welfare, but all I did was dwell on that one incident with those two girls that I mentioned to her. At that, she said she was just repeating what these girls had told her.

However, I admitted I've lied, acted out, wrote on desks, cheated on tests, and stole a copy of a World Geography exam, and she has forgiven me. Thus, I forgave her. She stated that I was the best monitor she ever had. In assembly, I hugged and kissed her and vice versa. No longer did I resent her, and she wasn't an old battle-ax anymore. We became friends for life. She told me I could write, call, or visit her at her home, which I did. She gave me colorful stationery at the end of the semester and sent me a New Year's card.

Mrs. Phillips is no longer here. She is missed and from time to time, I think lovely thoughts about her and am grateful to have known her.

THE CHEESE DOODLE LADY

Mrs. Schwartz, a dark-haired woman with glasses, turned out to be the brightest spot in my third year at school despite the disdainful remarks made of her by previous students. It was then I knew there was a God watching over me, contrary to my former school years.

One morning, while the class did their reading assignment, a guard from the upper grades brought in a boy named Steven who was reported for teasing me. The teacher reprimanded the boy and yelled in his face for about fifteen minutes. Then, she turned to the class with her finger pointed and reiterated for a long while, "Any boy or girl who teases Beth, their fathers will be called to school!" Each word she spoke was enunciated carefully and firmly. Then she called me out of the room and told me gently that if anyone teased me, I was to tell her. Just standing and watching her as she kneeled to comfort me, I said nothing but felt loved, cared for, and had nothing to worry about.

No one bothered me after that, except a girl, April, who sat next to me and made trouble for me. There was a popular fairy tale book I wanted from the class library entitled *After the Sunsets*. Everyone grabbed for it. When I told the teacher the children never gave me a chance, she held it for me on her desk. April, observing this, called me a bigshot, and I informed the teacher. She had April stand up in front of the class and scolded her. Her seat was changed, and she never upset me again.

Mrs. Schwartz made me her errand girl, for she had me deliver and pick up mail, correspondence, notes, attendance books, and letters throughout the school. A couple of times, she gave me the authority to call on children to hand out books and distribute scissors to those who did not have their own.

My teacher always made good but fair remarks on my report card. She noted that I was an obedient, quiet child who behaved well, but must learn to make friends and settle differences without getting upset. It was also stated that I was timid when speaking to an audience, but did well in all my subjects, except for math, in which I ended up receiving a 'satisfactory.'

Two of my achievements consisted of a weaving loom and stuffed doll, which were displayed in the window of the auditorium with other children's work, singled out as the best in their class. As the teacher led the class down the hall, she stopped and remarked, "Look at Beth's work. She worked very hard on her projects and that's why they were presented in the showcase." My classmates saw this, and I felt important, for Mrs. Schwartz showed her love and concern for me and felt I set a good example for the others to follow.

Also, Mrs. Schwartz became known as the 'Cheese Doodle Lady.' Whenever my mother packed a small bag of cheese doodles as a snack with my lunch, the teacher used to take some. When I forgot to bring them in one time, she playfully tapped me on the head and said, "Don't ever forget." It was very funny, and we had a good laugh.

Time went on, but I always remembered Mrs. Schwartz's kindness. It disturbed me when she retired, as I had no way of contacting her, but no one could take these pleasant memories away from me, for she was a teacher who believed in, cared for, and truly loved me for myself despite my emotional and social difficulties with other children.

I think of her often and miss her. Wherever she is, God bless her.

She proved to me that God exists.

WITH LOVE TO A VERY DEAR GRANDMOTHER

My greatest fear was the day my grandmother would die and I would not be there to say good-bye. I thought about it and had nightmares that I would be far away and not be there when she died, thus I promised myself I would be there.

I was my maternal grandmother's favorite, as well as the eldest of her five grandchildren. Ever since I could remember, there was always something waiting for me at her house.

"Where's my present?" I'd innocently ask, typical of a child.

When she came to my house, she would hand me a wrapped box and I would furiously rip off the paper, struggling with the scotch tape.

As a child, I spend countless hours with my grandmother, for she loved to tell stories. Once she told me how she helped a total stranger. "It's not what I did or who the person was, but I helped someone. I reached out and not only did she feel good, but I did too." From then on, I decided no act of kindness so small is ever wasted.

She listened when I tearfully told her about the cruel pranks and jokes the children played on me and the insensitive, callous teachers who did nothing to prevent the teasing. She handed me a tissue, took me to the bathroom, and washed my face while comforting me with her endearing expressions.

She believed I should do for others so I would not have the time to think of myself so much.

I learned that self-centered, egotistical people ranked lowest on a happiness scale. When one helps the less fortunate, one forgets his own troubles and has no time to wallow away in self-pity. One realizes how lucky he is and that nothing is as bad as they think. So many people have less.

"You're a lucky girl," my grandmother stated years ago. Back then, I did not believe her, but now I do. Millions have it worse, I discovered.

Also, more importantly, she told me to believe in myself. "You're smart, you're sweet, you're beautiful. Look in the mirror. Hold your head high like a queen." She often did this for she loved herself. She never went outside without lipstick and always wore a clean duster. Her clothes matched. At fourteen years old, she was a knockout with dark, wavy hair, dark black eyes, and a curvy figure, smoking a cigarette. All the boys were after her. She preferred older men. She found that boys her age were immature. She wished the same for me, for she mentioned that I had a complex. I did not like myself, she often stated, for I used to dwell on the past.

Throughout the years up until the time she died in April, thirty-one years ago, we exchanged cards, letters, and telephone calls. I sent her every greeting card there was—birthday, Mother's Day, Thanksgivings' Day, Valentine's Day, Chanukah, Passover, New Year's, and Grandparents' Day. I was the only grandchild who sent her the latter. My letters were like visits, she would say, for they consisted of several typewritten pages dealing with my job, friends, activities, movies, television shows, and most importantly—books. I was advised to read philosophical and psychological books rather than ones dealing with morbid subjects such as child abuse or the handicapped. Telephone calls always ended with "I love you." My grandmother was not a sentimentalist, but she did say it, and I know she meant and felt it. Also, she would call me "honey" and "bubala," an old Jewish expression. Even when she became ill in 1989, I would still say, "I love you," and she would return the greeting. I felt fine.

Nothing could have been worse than my grandmother's ordeal. She lingered on in body for a year and a half, but her mind went. Slowly, she was unable to take care of herself, became forgetful, and asked about my dead grandfather. One day, when I called her on the telephone, she did not know who I was. There had been a flicker, when my name was mentioned, but it was just a flicker that vanished forever. This hurt more than death, for my grandmother's mind was always sharp as a tack, and she always took excellent care of herself. It was just a matter of time. Friends agreed that her death was a blessing in disguise.

Services took place on a warm, sunny Friday afternoon in Long Island. Besides myself, my parents, brother, two cousins, mother's cousin and his wife, and uncle's widow were there to pay their respects. Few tears were shed. She slipped away peacefully in her sleep, for her heart stopped beating. I cried when her mind stopped functioning. I was angry and hurt. I wanted to scream and cry out, "Why God, why?" or slam something, but I did not. It was the end. I loved her, and I am sure she is looking down at me and knows how much I miss her.

Every time Mother's Day and Grandparents' Day roll around, or I see birthday cards to 'Grandmother,' I get an ache in my heart. I walk into a card store and see beautiful, flowery, colorful greeting cards say, 'To a very dear grandmother,' and I feel like I am going to cry, but I can't. I would run out of the store. No one must know or see. I know it is over, but the pain and sadness of seeing a loved one deteriorate before one's eyes is too deep for tears. However, she is now at peace in God's hands. Her suffering and pain are over. Life goes on. Tomorrow is a new day.

"Good-bye, Grandmother. I love you." Beth Carol.

LOVE AND HAPPINESS

Love is a mother who gives up her vacation to fly home—after repeatedly swearing she will never fly—on her birthday to take care of her adult daughter who isn't feeling well and takes her to the doctor.

Love is a mother defending her daughter against tormentors.

Love is a mother who tells her daughter to go outside with a stick to use against bullies.

Love is a mother who listens to her daughter when she is perturbed about past tribulations.

Love is a mother who makes telephone calls, visits, and writes letters supporting her daughter against cruel teachers, counselors, and vicious children, seeing that she is unharmed, well-protected, and happy.

Love is a father who reprimands and threatens harm to any child who hurts his daughter in any way.

Love is a father who stops everything to take his car out to drive his daughter anywhere she chooses.

Love is a father who, when he receives a call at work informing him of a problem, jumps in the car and is home in a flash.

Love is when a family sticks together during tragedy and collaborates with each other to solve problems.

Love is celebrating birthdays and graduations.

Love is my dog, * Heather, who always greeted me at the door.

Love is when Heather came over to me just like that, to be petted and to give me her paw.

Love is a stranger on the bus who gives a troubled young lady candy, sits by, listens to, and extends her hand to her.

Happiness is being productive and doing for others unselfishly.

Happiness is knowing you tried your best and being left unperturbed by others' disparaging remarks.

Happiness is belonging and being undemanding of others.

Happiness is loving and accepting yourself wholeheartedly—faults and all—regardless of what others think and feel.

Happiness is letting things slide and not sweating the small stuff.

Happiness is loving someone unconditionally by acknowledging and appreciating their positive points and overlooking and forgiving their negative ones.

Happiness is not caring who is right or wrong.

Happiness is spreading and sending love to your enemies and wishing them well.

Happiness is reading inspirational books such as *Chicken Soup for the Soul.*

And most of all, love and happiness are about being alive in spirit and mind, as well as in physical form.

Note: *My dog, Heather, passed away in 2003 after this first edition was published.

FORGIVENESS FOR OTHERS: OUR GIFT

"Forgive those who hurt you and forget to hurt them back" (author unknown), is a saying I feel applies to humankind today. Showing forgiveness to those who offend us is an admirable quality in a person. The books of Matthew, Luke, and Romans from the New Testament discuss forgiveness for others.

Matthew says to love your enemies and pray for them when they hurt you, for you will be acting as God's child, for God gives sunlight to good and evil. Luke says to love and do good to those who curse and persecute you and pray for them to be happy. Give them things you need for yourself and be compassionate. Do not expect to be repaid. It is better to give than to receive. Treat others the way you want to be treated. Romans also tell us to pray that God will bless your enemies. Do not condemn or pay back evil for evil. Two wrongs do not make a right. Getting even is a loser's game. In Norman Vincent Peale's *12 Steps for a Happy and Successful Life*, he mentions that Christ says to forgive seventy times seventy, if necessary. To be literal, that means four-thousand-and-nine-hundred times. It is prophesized that long before one has forgiven four-thousand-and-nine-hundred times, one will be free of all resentment. One will never be spiritually blessed until he forgives. This is a basic spiritual law. Good cannot flow to you unless it flows from you.

I feel when one has forgiveness in his heart, he will be very happy and live a good, long life, because he has found God within himself. People who cannot forgive get sick mentally and physically. Norman Vincent Peale called this dying from 'grudgitis.'

People get cancer, ulcers, and heart attacks from the lack of ability to forgive. People are committed to mental hospitals and institutions because they have never learned to forgive. They destroy themselves because forgiveness is a gift you give yourself. To forgive is to set a prisoner free and discover that prisoner was you. Only brave people know how to forgive. Cowards never forgive. It is not their nature.

We live in a world where people hurt each other—family members, friends, neighbors, employers, co-workers, teachers, colleagues, just to name a few. Norman Vincent Peale, Dr. Robert Schuller, Dr. Ruth Ross, Shakti Gawain, Harold Kushner, Terry Cole-Whittaker, and Lewis B. Smedes have authored books on forgiveness, which I have devoured immensely.

I have been trying for years to forgive those who have hurt me in the past. More than four decades ago, I just could not forgive. I wanted to, but felt I could never do it, and it killed me. In 1977, my mother told me to read Norman Vincent Peale's best-selling book, *The Power of Positive Thinking*. After I read a few pages, I felt lighter, relieved, and freed.

In 1971, when I was in group therapy, there was a girl my age who functioned as though she knew everything about everyone. She accused me of hating my mother and told her so, in addition to teasing me about a relative, R., whom I complained bitterly about. She maliciously and coyly asked me if I wanted to be like R. after I'd talk derogatorily about her and continually say, "I don't want to be like her." It happened that the girl's mother was in a mental hospital, her father abandoned her family, and her older brother antagonized and blamed her, thus he was not allowed to know where she was living, which was with different foster families—one of which hated her because of her religion. She stated all her relatives were poor, white trash. Friends told me to forgive her instead of hating her for teasing me about R. She needed sympathy, kindness, and understanding. Perhaps . . .

In 1975, I complained bitterly to a friend about a high school guidance counselor who was extremely vicious toward me. Though she sympathized with me, she told me to wish her well. I looked at her aghast and said, "I hope she drops dead!" Now when I think of it, my friend was right. I am no longer angry with the counselor. I am not saying I have forgotten, but I forgave her, and it no longer hurts.

In the same year, I told my cousin, Michele, about a girl I befriended when I first moved in who was extremely nice and friendly at first, but suddenly stopped our relationship by siding with two girls who told malicious lies about me, by calling me a liar and being sarcastic when I defended myself. My cousin said to me, "Why don't you call her and ask her to go to a movie?" I was indignant, for I could not believe what I was hearing. Michele said I was being childish and foolish. I did not think so then, but now I understand.

Another time in high school, a girl tried to make trouble for me, and I held a grudge against her for two years. Suddenly, one day, I said "Hello!" to her. I do not know why, but she said, "Hi, Beth." It was hard to believe. She signed my yearbook and graduation hat, and I am not saying she is my life-long friend, but we got along well after that and talked only of pleasant things.

In 1972, I met a friend, Marilyn, in Brooklyn College whom I knew in Midwood High School. I complained about girls we knew who had maltreated me, and I told her if I ever saw them again, I swore I'd kill them. At that, Marilyn said quietly, "Don't you think you should forgive and forget?"

A girl in junior high school pretended to be my friend one minute, and then the next minute she did such things as spill milk in my lunch, pull my handkerchief off, hide and knock my books around, and steal money from me. Years later, we had a nice, long talk, and we spoke only of pleasant things.

Another example is with a teacher I had in the seventh grade whom everyone hated. She yelled at me constantly in front of the class, and once she grabbed me by the wrist unjustly. Believe me, it hurt, and I swore I would never forgive her, so I went around school saying ugly and terrible things and authored a story about her.

You could tell I hated her, but later I saw that she had a good side, and she really did like me. I felt warmth and love and wished her well. Sadly, she passed on years later.

There was an incident with a 'cab' driver and two police officers where I was completely humiliated and every so often this upsets me, thus I use the affirmation which I say and write from time to time, "I, Beth Carol, fully and freely forgive that driver and policemen for the trouble they caused me." There are times when I would want to scream and get even, but I think about forgiving and it no longer hurts. While doing visualization and meditation, I say, "I forgive and release you. Go your way, and I'll go mine. God bless you."

At times, I'd get upset over unpleasant events that occurred in the past with cruel teachers, an abusive camp counselor, and any peers. I would think of getting even by harassing them on the telephone and writing threatening letters, making them pay for what they did to me, but there is an expression that the Bible mentions that I should quote, "Love your enemies, bless them that curse you, do good to them that hate you, and pray for them when they despitefully use and persecute you." Also, I repeat the affirmation, "I, Beth Carol, fully and freely forgive those who have hurt me in the past." I even wrote letters (unmailed) forgiving them.

What really hurt were issues that occurred in my family such as mistrust, unjust criticism, and false accusations, but with the help of knowing God was within me, I am learning to forgive.

There are other personal instances, but I would like to mention others forgiving. A woman loves her husband, and he 'loves' her, but he goes off to war and impregnates a young woman, and the wife supports the child after its mother dies. A man wishes his rebellious daughter well. A pope who was almost killed goes to the jail where his would-be assassin is and prays for him. A couple whose promising son is killed by another couple, befriend the couple. A woman whose family was killed by the Nazis, becomes friends with them.

Also, I read Wayne W. Dyer's books, where he writes about growing up wondering about his father whom he never saw. Melvin Lyle Dyer was a drunkard, abusive toward his wife and family, never did honest work, was in constant trouble with the law, and even served time in prison. Wayne W. Dyer had been dominated by his father's abandonment for years and had the need to contact him. When he matured, he discovered his father died and visited his grave. He said at his father's gravesite, "I forgive you. I send you love." His hatred ended, and his life changed for the better. He authored best-selling books, appeared on television, lectured, and became famous.

Another person I feel has been extremely forgiving is my former employer, Mel. I have worked for him longer than at any job I ever had. He could have fired me at any time, but he did not, for I have been a great problem to him. I have misbehaved, made repeated costly errors in my work, and have stolen from him on many occasions. What he felt was hurt, because he is a person who has always treated people the way he wants to be treated. However, he forgave me many times. I feel that despite his edginess and short-temperedness, he is a saint, for he has God in him and has the ability to forgive.

My two bus friends, Gladys and Dorothy, are also fitting examples of forgiveness. Gladys mentioned that her mother preferred her brother to her, blamed her for being born, and named her after her estranged husband's ex-girlfriend. Now, she has buried the hatchet and is close to both her mother and brother.

Dorothy was the odd one out of her family. She had a troublemaking sister whom her mother favored over her and her other siblings. Dorothy said years later that her mother explained to her and her siblings that it was because she felt this sister was weak. Dorothy disagreed, but said, "In her mind, she was right." And Dorothy became closest to this sister more than her other siblings and said, "I love my sister despite her weakness."

When we forgive others, we are doing the Lord's work, for God loves us all and rewards us when we forgive. I am trying very hard to instill this quality within me. It is not easy, but I read uplifting books and repeatedly play tapes about God and forgiveness and do affirmations daily, telling me to forgive as I mentioned earlier. Some of them are quotes from the Bible.

Beginning with a quote, I will also end with one from Lewis B. Smedes' book *Forgive and Forget the Hurts We Do Not Deserve*. "When we forgive, we ride the crest of love's cosmic wave; we walk in stride with God, and we heal the hurts we never deserved."

PART TWO:

TWO NOVELLAS

THESE THREE

CHAPTER ONE

It was a typical turbulent night in the Johnstone's bedroom.

First a vase flew, then a lamp. A slap landed across Marion's face. She screamed.

"Shut up, bitch! Get outta here!" Victor yelled at his wife. She tried to hide her face with her hands while she crouched in the corner of the bedroom in her white lace slip.

"Please!" she begged. "Please, don't hit me again!"

Victor stood six feet tall and weighed more than two hundred pounds. He poured whiskey into his small glass. Then, he quickly gulped it down.

"Go back to your lover, you fuckin' tramp!" he yelled angrily. "Run to your architect, Howard or Harry, what's-his-name!"

"Harold," Marion corrected quietly.

Grabbing her arm, Victor haughtily spat out, "So you admit it! You do, don't you?"

Still terrified and crouching from fear of her husband, Marion managed to say, "What about your affairs with Sherry and that blonde waitress, Marie? What about Rita, and Diane? Don't they count?"

While tightening his grip on her arm, he slapped her viciously across the face. Marion sobbed hysterically, her face buried in her hands. She fell to the floor. Victor smiled, standing over her.

"Get your things and get out! Don't come back, you stupid little bitch!" he warned. Marion got up slowly and staggered across the room, holding her bruised face.

She slowly turned toward Victor, adding firmly in a deep voice, "You killed my little girl—little Arlena." Her eyes glared at him.

"You're half right, you stupid cunt . . . about her being your little girl."

"She was yours, too," Marion carefully added.

Victor ran to her and put his fist near her jaw. "That brat was no daughter of mine, that retarded, bitchy idiot," he spat out.

"No, she wasn't," she protested. "She was a person with a brain injury. And even if she were . . ."

"Don't contradict me, you stupid little bitch." Victor reached for his bottle and drank some before striking his wife again.

Marion said calmly, "You've hit me for the last time." She proceeded to pack.

"Where will you go?" Victor asked mockingly, expecting her answer.

"I don't think I have to tell you. You know I intend to terminate this marriage . . . if it's all the same to you." Marion continued packing while Victor watched.

He loved her once, she knew, as she had cared for him. They were barely twenty then, but they were very much in love. Marion worked as a salesclerk and attended college classes when she could. She had large, bright brown eyes and wavy blonde hair. Victor fondly told her she was as slim and graceful as a bird.

Victor once had a successful career, but after thirty years of marriage, his lingerie business went bankrupt. Meanwhile, Marion became a successful teacher-psychologist. Her success made him complain that he was a failure as a man.

During the first few years of marriage, Marion gave birth to three sons, all stillborn. Disappointed, Victor constantly belittled his wife. He also considered her a failure as a woman. He wanted a son badly.

A year later, she had a beautiful, blonde, curly-haired daughter, who had a brain injury. Marion worked to support the three of them. When the infant was a baby, no one suspected anything was wrong. She walked, sat, ate, talked, and developed like other children. When she was about five years old and started kindergarten, her problems became noticeable.

She couldn't learn to read, write, or recognize the letters of her own name, although she could count to 1,000 and could recite the letters of the alphabet and their sounds. When quizzed orally in science or social studies, she was ahead of her peers.

Still, she was unable to make sense out of symbolic language—anything printed or written. Though she was allowed into the first grade, she was retained for an extra year. There was no progress.

At the same time, Victor's business began to fail. He constantly vented his frustrations on his wife and daughter, beating them both. Sometimes he gave Marion a black eye. Other times, he hit her so badly she looked like a bloody pulp. There were times that Marion lay on the floor in a heap.

One night, Victor went into Arlena's room while she was sleeping and hit her head with a baseball bat. They took Arlena to their physician. Marion, afraid of her husband, told the doctor Arlena fell and hit her head against a wall.

The doctor didn't pursue the matter, serious as it was. He said the child was unconscious. It was a matter of time before her life would be over.

Arlena lay in a coma for two years. When she finally died, Marion and Victor buried her in a small plot behind their house. Marion mourned the loss of her child deeply for years, but she did nothing to escape her violent husband.

Victor's business worsened. He continued to drink, go out with other women, and beat Marion. His sweet, passive wife bore the abuse for twenty years after Arlena's death, working until she completed her Ph.D. Marion decided to instruct children with emotional disturbances and brain injuries a few miles from her home.

There, Marion met Harold Cummings, an architect.

Harold was a quiet, dark-haired man, himself divorced after twenty-five years in a turbulent marriage.

Harold's wife, Betty, left him when she decided she no longer wanted to be married. She opened a small dress boutique in Chicago, where she expected to rediscover who she was. Since their two children, a son and a daughter, were grown and on their own, there were no obstructions to ending their marriage. Betty wanted out. Harold agreed. Their arrangement remained friendly.

During the last few years of the marriage, Betty became a cold, unresponsive wife. The children were old enough to cope with the change, and they still saw and called both parents regularly.

Alan, twenty-three, was a resident doctor. Alice, twenty-one, was in college studying fashion design. She was a Dean's List student and President of the Student Body.

* * * * *

When Harold was laying out plans for the new school, he met Marion. Their relationship began with coffee and cake, then progressed to dinner. Despite that first involvement, she wouldn't sleep with Harold until a year later.

Harold confronted Marion's guilt about their affair. "Marion, honey, from what you've told me, he frequently sleeps with other women."

Marion couldn't answer. She knew Harold was right. She wondered, 'Why shouldn't I? If Victor had meaningless flings with anyone available, why shouldn't I have a relationship with a warm, kind man who loves me and treats me with respect?'

Though Victor still drank excessively and had sex with other women, Marion stayed married to him. No one else understood her behavior. In fact, she didn't understand it herself. She knew she loved Harold, and he loved her. The feelings between them were deep. Still, she felt morally obligated to Victor.

* * * * *

One year later, Marion's life changed for the better. After that last relentless beating, Marion coolly decided to dissolve their marriage. She took back her family name, Strauss. She tried to forget Victor and her life with him. She moved into Harold's spacious home.

After a few weeks together, Harold and Marion went to a professional photographer to get their pictures taken. They had copies made in diverse sizes and displayed them all over the house. They even had one enlarged that showed Harold holding Marion tightly around her waist. They put it over their bed. They purchased a bungalow in the Catskills, where they went each summer. They boated, fished, and played bridge. They swam in the community pool, and sometimes took walks in the woods to watch the animals chase each other and play together. They drove to the beach to collect shells, and they often rented a boat and went sailing.

Harold treated Marion with profound respect. He bought her fine clothes and expensive jewelry to show he loved her. Since both were professionals, they hired household help and shared the responsibilities, but he made sure she was comfortable—even spoiled.

He always went along when she wanted to go to a particular event. She particularly loved lectures about psychology and education. Harold accompanied her agreeably. She also liked flea markets and garage sales, to which Harold went along. They both enjoyed movies.

Except when they worked, they always spent their leisure time together. On quiet days at home, Marion insisted on making Harold's favorites: lasagna, lobster, and veal. She loved cooking for him.

She loved him deeply. They disagreed and argued at times, but once Marion put on a sexy nightgown, the fight usually disintegrated as though nothing happened. It was forgotten. They cuddled in bed and kissed, then made love. Neither held a grudge.

Finally, Harold and Marion decided to pool their money for a cruise to Europe. They were tired of the city and wanted to try something new. They planned a six-week vacation in December and January, made their reservations, and were off. They enjoyed seeing historical sites, eating new foods, buying souvenirs, and taking endless pictures. They had an enjoyable time—a new adventure.

Harold and Marion enjoyed their life of bliss, together.

* * * * *

Marion met Harold's children, Alice and Alan, a few weeks before their first summer at the bungalow.

The women enjoyed each other's company. They took long walks and spent hours talking about life.

Alan also got along well with Marion, although his shyness kept him from saying much to her. Marion was interested, but because Alan was distant, she didn't initiate conversation.

"You should be proud of your children," Marion told Harold after meeting them for the first time. "Alice is open, vivacious, and personable. We have great talks. Was she always like that?"

Harold laughed. "Always! She was always outgoing. She's talked to everyone since she was a little girl. Alan's different. He's a good kid, but he's introverted . . . like Betty. He's been a loner most of his life. He studies and works, and not much else. He feels close to Betty. I don't mind. As I said, he's a good boy."

CHAPTER TWO

"Do you love me, my darling?" Harold asked breathlessly one morning six years after they moved in together.

Marion and Harold lay in bed, with Harold squeezing Marion's breasts from behind. Marion kissed him gently then slowly climbed out of bed wearing a silky, transparent, black lace nightgown Harold bought her for her last birthday.

Harold grabbed her gently and attempted another kiss. She reciprocated with an embrace. Suddenly, the telephone rang. Their lovemaking was undaunted by the interruption. The telephone rang repeatedly.

As Harold caressed her, Marion interrupted quietly. "Honey, I think I should answer it."

Harold reluctantly released her from his gentle embrace, and she reached for the receiver.

"Hello," she said. There was a pause while she listened. "Oh," she said simply.

"I have to go," she told Harold, "It's the school, and they say it's important. I'm sorry, honey."

Late afternoon when she returned, she saw Harold sitting on the sofa reading the newspaper. He looked up at her.

"What is it, honey?" he asked.

"They're cutting back on funds," she said sadly. "They've let me go."

"Oh, Marion!" Harold was shocked. He put his newspaper down on the couch and asked, "What will you do? Do you want to stop working for a while, or do you want to go into private practice? We could . . ."

"They've found me another job . . . in a regular junior high school," she explained.

"What will you do there? Your job is instructing children with brain injuries and emotional issues," he protested.

"I'll still be doing that."

"Really? How?" he asked.

"I'll be a resource teacher. I'll teach a couple of special education students in regular programs," she explained.

"It sounds interesting," Harold admitted.

Marion frowned. "I don't know if I can do it."

"What do you mean? You've instructed special children for years," he pointed out.

"Not in a regular school," Marion said. "The children I'm used to teaching were never in regular classrooms."

"What's the difference?" he said.

Marion pondered his remark. "I don't know exactly," she mused. "The job sounds more complicated. There's little control over the rest of their school experience."

A week later, Marion was to start her new teaching position. She had met with Mr. Sam Marshall, the principal, the day before to describe the duties and responsibilities that her new position entailed. She had to read and sign contracts regarding her new position. She wanted to make sure she understood what was required of her.

She was to start the next morning, so she set her alarm clock earlier. She believed in punctuality. It was her first day and she wanted to make a good first impression. However, during the night, she inadvertently knocked the clock over and awakened on her own just in time.

"Oh my gosh, it's almost eight o'clock! I've got to get to the school by ten. It's an hour's drive. I'll have to skip breakfast."

Harold reached for her. She leaned toward him, smiled at him on the bed, and kissed him. He ran his fingers through her hair.

"I love you, Marion," he announced abruptly but gently.

A pained look crossed her face. Her eyes filled with tears and she turned away from him.

"What is it, honey?" He studied her with concern.

She shook her head, her back to him. "I've got to go."

She stood, but he again reached for her. She ignored his touch and dressed.

"Honey, I know something's wrong. Is it me?" he questioned.

Still dressing yet not facing him, she shook her head. "No," she replied quietly.

"Look, Marion, I've known you for six years . . ."

"It's not that," Marion replied. "It's difficult for me to say it, but I do love you, too. When you said it to me . . . I mean, I know you do, but . . ."

"But what?" he led on.

"I don't know." She looked down.

Harold climbed out of bed and put his arms around her from behind.

"Please, Harold. This is difficult enough." She turned. "Please," she said calmly. "I must go." She continued dressing, so Harold backed away from her slowly, watching her curiously.

When ready, Marion said quietly, "I must go."

Harold grabbed her and held her tightly, kissing her lips passionately.

Touching him gently, she said, "Please, Harold . . ."

He released her reluctantly.

She reached for her handbag, then prepared to leave. "Good-bye Harold." She gave him one last peck.

"Bye, Marion, darling," he said as she walked out.

* * * * *

As Marion drove down the road, tears blinded her bright brown eyes. She remembered the scene she and Harold had in the house. She loved Harold, but she felt uncomfortable when he came on so strongly, verbalizing his love. What about me? I love him, but what's he asking for? Does he want a commitment? I don't know if I'm ready to promise everything to him. I suffered from one abusive marriage—am I willing to try again? I don't know what to think or do. I don't trust what might happen after the marriage vows.

There were few cars on the road that morning. She missed the morning rush hour, so she assumed that was the reason the road was uncrowded. It was easy for Marion to drive and ponder her relationship with Harold. She loved him, but she wasn't ready for a permanent commitment. Marion didn't want to face the consequences of another binding marriage.

She arrived at her new job. It wasn't an impressive school. The building was old and dilapidated, and it had a poor reputation. Although it was a standard public junior high school, many of the students were considered lazy, slovenly, dirty, unkempt, and uninterested in learning. Marion wasn't pleased. From what she heard, the school was also poorly run.

When she entered the building, she suddenly felt ill. The floors were cracked and worn. The furniture was decaying and the paint on the walls was peeling.

Marion looked around. She heard a few faint voices.

Suddenly, a stout, tall woman with closely cropped red hair walked up to Marion.

"Doctor Strauss?" the woman inquired.

Marion turned. "Yes?"

"I'm Flora Burg. Come with me." The woman spoke without emotion. Marion followed her down the corridor into her office.

"Have a seat, Dr. Strauss," Flora said flatly. Marion obediently sat, following the woman's orders as though she were a young child.

"As you already know, Dr. Strauss, you'll teach a couple of students who have serious problems. You'll have two children. We feel they may benefit from your help—and I do mean may. Only God knows how much you could actually do for them. As far as I'm concerned, I don't believe in all this publicity. I don't see any sense for a resource teacher attempting to make these children normal."

"Frankly, I think the program's a waste of valuable time and money, but Samuel Marshall, our principal, thought it would be a good experiment. I don't know why, to tell you the honest-to-God truth."

Ms. Burg went to her desk, reached for two files, and handed them to Marion. Before Marion could make any effort to read them, Flora said, "Those are about your two resource students. God knows what you can do. Good luck," she offered wearily.

Outside the office, a piercing scream sounded. Marion and Flora turned. Marion was perplexed.

Flora sighed tiredly as she shook her head. "Oh, no, not Marilyn again."

"Marilyn?" Marion repeated.

The screaming became louder. Flora opened the office door and hurried out. Marion followed. She saw a girl with long, straight blonde hair run down the stairs, shrieking hysterically as though someone was chasing her.

"Marilyn, come back here now!" an aide shouted after the teen.

Flora turned to Marion. "That's one of your charges. Now you know what I mean."

"Where is she going?" Marion asked.

Flora shrugged. "To the girls' room, as usual. She locks herself in. Probably someone teased her or did something to her. Who knows?" She shrugged tiredly.

The aide banged on the door furiously and yelled again. "Marilyn! Come out this minute or you'll be sorry!"

Only silence followed.

"I'll call your mother!" the aide threatened firmly.

The door immediately opened.

"Now, young lady, get back to class. No more repeat episodes, understand?" She glared powerfully at the child.

"Donna Cooper kicked me!" Marilyn screamed.

The aide paid her complaint no heed. "I don't care," she stated arrogantly. "Get back to class, and I mean it!"

"That always works," Flora told Marion.

"Really?" Marion remarked. "Why?"

"You see, Dr. Strauss, the girl's mother is a powerful woman in this community, especially in this school. In fact, she's one of our biggest contributors. Not only that, but she's also brutal and domineering toward Marilyn, so the girl is simply terrified of her. When Joan Wentworth hears any negative reports about her daughter . . ." Flora stopped.

Marion timidly asked, "What does she do?"

"She beats her . . . almost every day, as soon as she comes home from school."

Marion was shocked. What kind of woman could treat her own child like that?

"But why?" Marion wondered.

Flora shrugged. "Who knows?" She shook her head.

"Ms. Burg, you mean you're aware of this child being abused and you haven't done anything to stop it?"

Shrugging, Flora explained, "Look, Dr. Strauss, I need this job. Everyone who works here depends on this woman. If word went out that Joan Wentworth was abusive, then we'd lose her. Everyone here would be on the street."

Marion couldn't believe the situation. She considered it unreal and inhumane.

Flora said, "Well, there is your first charge—Marilyn Wentworth."

Turning back to the office, Flora started to mention Marion's other student.

Suddenly, a bang sounded loudly. Marion jumped.

"Leave me the fuck alone!" a young boy shrieked.

"Oh," Flora sighed, then turned to Marion. "That's your other charge. He sees a therapist every morning from nine to ten. He's still the same, regardless."

The two women turned to see the boy throwing his books around, still screaming at the aide. He ran upstairs. The aide shouted after him, "Brent, stop that shouting or I'll have your father take you home!"

Flora told Marion with a long, tired sigh, "His father is like Joan Wentworth."

"Really?" Marion said, irritated.

Ignoring Marion's remark, Flora said, "Those two are your charges. Good luck!" She showed no trace of emotion or kindness.

Marion stood in a fog when Flora left her at the office door. She continued to ponder her position. She would teach the two children in the afternoon. Marilyn would attend regular classes—English, mathematics, social studies, and science—in the morning. She would be excused from physical education, art, and music to work with Marion after lunch.

Brent was suspended from attending regular high school because of his violent temper, which frightened other students and teachers. A private tutor in the mornings taught his required subjects. In the afternoon, he would be with Marion.

CHAPTER THREE

"How are you, Marilyn?" Marion smiled warmly at the girl as she walked into the classroom wearing an expensive, beautiful lilac floral lace dress. "I'm glad you're my student."

Marilyn did not return her teacher's greeting.

Instantly, Marion realized she asked the wrong question. But before she had a chance to apologize, Marilyn exploded out of her seat, throwing her textbooks at Marion.

Marilyn screamed, "I hate women! I hate women!" She raced around the room in a frenzy, shoving books off the shelves and throwing them toward Marion, who stood staring at her.

Marion remained calm, saying nothing.

Instantly, Brent threw his physics book directly at Marilyn.

"Jesus Christ!" he yelled, jumping from his chair. "What the fuck?"

"Shut the hell up!" Marilyn screamed back at him.

"No!" he shouted back. Seeing that Marion didn't react, he asked, "What's wrong with you, lady? Aren't you going to do something?"

Marilyn continued to scream hysterically. "I hate women!" She sobbed, "Everyone lies to me. Women hate me!"

"I don't," Marion spoke sincerely. Marion went over to the girl and attempted to gently button Marilyn's dress to comfort her, but she jerked away. "Please, come over and sit down." Marion attempted to lead her to her seat. "It's time to work now."

Marilyn's cheeks flamed. She clenched her fists and screamed at Marion. "I hate you!" She continued to sob while tears streamed down her face. "Goddamn you," she spat at Marion, "you're like everyone else trying to dominate me and telling me what to do. Well, I hate you! You hate me, too! You're just like her! You'll do what she does!"

"Who?" Marion asked finally.

"My mother!" Marilyn answered angrily.

Marion stood watching the girl. She said nothing.

"Damn you!" Marilyn screamed out again.

Marion tried to stroke the girl again, but once more she jerked away.

"Don't touch me . . . ever! You're like her!"

"Your mother?" Marion reiterated flatly.

"Yes!" Marilyn shouted. Marion stood in the same spot, saying nothing. "I hate my life! I wish I were dead!" the girl screamed.

Marilyn dashed toward the door and opened it furiously. It made a loud bang when she ran out, screaming uncontrollably down the hall. Marion quickly turned to Brent.

"Will you be, okay? I'll be back," Marion promised. He briefly nodded without looking up from his books.

Doors banged open in the hall. Other teachers and students entered the hall as well, murmuring.

"Crazy girl!" one student mocked.

One teacher whispered loudly to another, "It's one of those moronic students from across the hall. I don't know why those children are allowed at this school with normal students. They're nuts. Something ought to be done about it."

Marion turned toward them but said nothing.

"Hey, crazy lady bitch!" a boy jeered at Marion. She ignored him.

Flora Burg stomped down the hall angrily. "What's going on?" she demanded to know.

One teacher shrugged. "Who knows? Someone from her crazy room!" She pointed at Marion, coolly.

Flora turned toward Marion furiously. "Dr. Strauss, I thought you were watching your kids. They can't take care of themselves, you know. That's your job. Look, Doctor, you were hired to help those kids. Now look how you're managing. Excellent job!" she remarked sarcastically. "Great job! Was that Marilyn?"

Marion nodded. She was too stunned at the prevailing attitudes to react.

"You're supposed to watch her. Look how you're doing it . . . letting her scream down the hall and disrupt the school."

Flora went on. "I want you to know this—you'd better learn to control those kids. If you don't . . ." She didn't finish her sentence but left it hanging like a thread.

Marion spoke up. "I'll take care of the problem. Let me do it my way. I think I can help her."

"Okay," Flora said sternly. "If you don't there's going to be one big problem—for you."

"Let me take care of it," Marion repeated softly. "Okay?"

Marion and Flora walked together looking for Marilyn.

When they reached the stairs, Flora told Marion, "She's in the bathroom again. Let me handle this. I know what to do."

"No," Marion objected gently. "Let me . . . okay?"

"Look, I know how to handle this girl," Flora grew firm.

Marion stood firmly as well. "Ms. Burg, Marilyn is my student now. I think you should let me try. Please," she implored.

Flora shrugged. "Okay." She left. Marion slowly walked downstairs to the restroom. When she got there, she knocked gently on the door.

"Marilyn?" she called.

She heard only silence.

Marion continued, "Look, Marilyn, I know you're there."

Still, silence greeted her.

Marion tried opening the door, but it was locked.

"Marilyn, please come out," Marion implored once more.

More silence followed.

"If you don't come out, you'll have to listen to me." Marion placed a chair near the bathroom door, then sat down. "You know, Marilyn, I had a daughter once . . . like you. In fact, she'd be your age now, if she were living. She was a lot like you. She had some problems. No one understood them. She was called all kinds of names and teased."

"I'm going to let you know something about my personal life I've never told anyone. My ex-husband, her father, couldn't accept our little girl, so he killed her. I never forgot that, but since you've come along, I feel more in control. Do you understand what I mean? I mean . . . I could help you. I think I could. I couldn't help my own daughter, but God is giving me a second chance by bringing you into my life." She took a breath. "You mention your problems . . . your mother, for instance. For me, it was my ex-husband. There's always something with everybody. So, darling, don't think you're alone. You're not. Really, you aren't. I believe I could help you. Please, Marilyn, let me try to reach you."

The door slowly opened. Marilyn walked over. Softly and quietly, she said, "Marion." A smile slowly crossed Marilyn's tear-stained face.

"Do you love me?" Marilyn asked, unbelieving.

"Yes," she answered, trying not to cry. "Yes," she quickly repeated.

The tears were coming. Marion tried to brush them away, with no success.

Marilyn suddenly put both her arms around Marion's neck and kissed her cheek gently.

"I love you, too," Marilyn whispered shyly.

Marion put her arms around the girl. Her tears fell quietly.

"I'm sorry," Marilyn said.

Marion patted her back gently. Still embracing the girl, she added, "Don't worry, honey. I'll help you."

"You won't tell my mother?" she pleaded.

"No," Marion agreed. "I won't tell your mother. Trust me."

CHAPTER FOUR

"I need to find out more about Marilyn and Brent," Marion said to Harold as he kissed the back of her neck.

Marilyn was an attractive, blonde-haired child of fifteen, with large, deep, dark, angry eyes. She was a severely battered child, abused by her mother. Her IQ was superior; however, when she five years old, it was discovered she had a marginal brain injury.

Through elementary school, she struggled. She tried to read and write but couldn't. She visualized letters and numbers jumbled up and couldn't make sense out of anything symbolic.

The doctors tried to explain her situation to her parents. Her father accepted her limitations, but her mother refused to believe there was anything wrong with her child. She complained that Marilyn simply didn't study enough and goofed off. Her mother believed she didn't try, and that she simply didn't put in any effort.

Marilyn's mother was not the girl's biological parent. Doctors had diagnosed that Joan was unable to have a baby the natural way, so she and her husband had paid a woman a handsome sum of money to have the baby for them. No evidence of any problems was conspicuous at birth. Her birth mother was a short, blonde-haired person. As far as anyone knew, no health problems were ever evident in her; she was physically, mentally, and emotionally stable.

Surprisingly however, three years after Marilyn's birth, Joan found herself pregnant and gave birth to an eight-pound, four-ounce blue-eyed boy with light brown curls and a little round face, whom she named Randall.

Joan was a domineering mother, like her own father had been. Joan was a Daddy's Girl, who worked hard to get his love. She did anything, right or wrong, that made him love her. She hated her own cold, cruel, apathetic, uncaring mother, who preferred her highly educated professional son who, in her mind, could do no wrong.

Joan had repeated her own mother's parenting pattern. Her son became the apple of her eye. He always received the highest marks in his class, as well as school awards. He had no problems in school whatsoever. He was her world.

Joan took out all her frustrations on Marilyn once the girl started having problems in school. When her father had died, Joan inherited his business and his money, but she also inherited his temperament. Joan was the president of numerous organizations and gave freely to charities, but her largest contribution went to resource students like Marilyn.

Joan was considered beautiful. Tall and slim, her dark, thick hair would be always carefully styled. She had piercing dark eyes. She made sure she got what she wanted, or there was trouble.

Gerald, Marilyn's father, was a mild-mannered, good-natured, shy, introverted man who couldn't manage his wife. He enjoyed working with his hands as a mechanic in a garage, which Joan insisted on buying an interest in.

Everyone loved Gerald Wentworth, but Joan was feared. She had become what was important to her—respected and wealthy. As a result, Marilyn developed deep emotional problems, compounded by her learning disabilities.

After harsh abuse, Marilyn suffered a severe mental disturbance. She developed poor impulse control, displayed obsessional thinking, had paranoid ideas, and displayed inappropriate behavior in public places. Her mood swings were abnormal, and she showed evidence of gross thought content disorder and irrelevant speech.

She was diagnosed with schizophrenia—chronic undifferentiated type. She became known for violent and sudden outbursts of temper, talking to herself, and biting her hands. When she wasn't doing those things, she acted silly, and made nonsensical remarks. Her speech was redundant, and she laughed aloud at the wrong time.

From the time she was nine, she was in and out of therapy—some of which helped, but only temporarily. Medication was tried, but it was unsuccessful. Her social life was zero, so she spent her free time listening to music.

The only reason Marilyn remained in this school program was because of Joan's contributions. For years in elementary school, teachers obediently passed her to the next grade. Later, classmates taunted her when she failed to keep up academically. When she entered junior high, she was detained three times. A special school placement would be arranged if Marilyn failed the seventh grade again.

Brent had no biological learning disabilities. He was evaluated when he was three years old and he was found to have a validated IQ of 188. His marks in school were excellent, and he was especially proficient in the pure and applied sciences and math.

Computers, clocks, televisions, radios, anything mechanical or electronical interested him. He spent his entire allowance on such devices and took them apart to figure out how each part operated. However, he considered school a waste of time. He felt he knew more than his teachers, so he didn't let anyone reach him.

Brent didn't allow anyone to touch him. He was opposed to physical contact with people and was often violent when threatened. The episode that first afternoon underscored that. He was sarcastic and defensive.

As a teenager, he still had a naivete characteristic of a child. He exhibited frequent narcissistic preoccupation and infantile omnipotence, plus poor self-identity and self-esteem. He couldn't cope with his own fluctuating moods of anxiety and anger effectively enough to function in a regular classroom.

Brent was a tall, sandy-blonde-haired, dark-eyed boy of seventeen who wore wire-rimmed glasses. He was good looking, although always angry. He never dated or had any friends. He stayed in his room day after day, reading physics, calculus, and chemistry books.

His communication with others was minimal. He and his parents hardly talked with each other. His mother tried, but his father never did. Brent was a loner and liked it that way.

Brent's father, Marvin, was a brilliant, successful surgeon. After graduating from New York Medical School at the top one percent of his class at age twenty-one, he began his career. When he learned his son was gifted, his resentment and jealousy caused him to badger Brent to bolster his own insecurity. He was a loud man who intimidated everyone and demanded he was right about everything.

Brent's mother, Clara, was a small, meek, passive woman with faded blonde hair worn in a hairnet. She loved working in her garden growing herbs, fruits, and vegetables. She was also active in her church and volunteered her time at a nursing home. She gave up her job as a nursery school director and teacher at her husband's insistence to raise their son. Marvin resented having a working wife, and a professional at that who was educated. He hated competition.

Brent was put in Marion's class as a last resort. If he didn't improve, his father intended to institutionalize him.

After Marion read the case histories of her two new students, she considered the comparisons. Joan and Marvin were alike—brutal and domineering, while their spouses were meek and good-natured. Both children were extremely bright but severely disturbed. Both were angry at their parents, at the world, and at those who tried relentlessly to help them but couldn't. They were emotionally and physically abused adolescents who came from wealthy backgrounds—two innocent children living in purgatory, struggling for places in a society too harsh for the weak, troubled, or tormented.

Marion sighed.

She mused, here are two children, considered hopeless cases, looking for love—love they never found. Both were shut off from beauty and exposed to nothing but life's cruelties.

Marion wanted to give them the love no one else ever gave them. They were problems turned over to Marion as a last hope. No one else wanted them or knew what to do with them. They were Marion's responsibility. Her job was to help them cope—to live and function in a world that prized accomplishments and scorned those who were different. Marion admitted it wouldn't be easy. It would take a long time, but she was determined. She wouldn't fail—she knew it. Marilyn and Brent would be a challenge, but Marion vowed to succeed.

* * * * *

She shared her day with Harold that night, describing the beautiful, deeply tortured Marilyn who could not read or write, and whom she instantly loved as if she were her own child, her own little girl, Arlena.

Brent, on the other hand, she found completely cold, oblivious to everything and everyone. Marion recognized his extreme intelligence, ruggedly handsome stature, and distant disposition.

She loved them both and wanted to take them to her heart. She decided she had at least marginally reached Marilyn, who showed potential and was affectionate. She hoped she could do as well with Brent. She didn't know for sure, but she wasn't willing to admit defeat.

Harold fondled her gently. Marion let him, but she continued talking about Marilyn.

"She's like my little girl," she mused. "Marilyn is sweet, gentle, and innocent."

Harold put his arms around Marion's waist and pulled her toward him on the bed. He covered her face with kisses and ran his hand through her hair tenderly.

"I'm happy for you, Marion," he whispered. "You had an interesting day. It's a shame, though, about those kids. They face such problems. I wish I could help in some way."

Marion kissed him back. "You don't have to. Just care and be here for me, okay?"

He took her gently in his arms. Feeling her soft, sweet breasts, he made passionate love to her.

CHAPTER FIVE

"Hello, Brent," Marion greeted as he walked through the classroom door.

Brent did not return her greeting. He sat down with his chemistry book and began studying various equations and formulas.

Marilyn skipped in gleefully and smiled. "Hello, Marion." She turned toward Brent and greeted him as well, but he didn't answer. "I said, 'Hello,'" she repeated. Still, he didn't answer. She turned to Marion. "Why doesn't he answer me?" she asked.

Marion wearily advised, "Sit down, Marilyn. It's time to start your classwork. You have a test in math tomorrow."

Marilyn didn't budge.

"Marion, why won't he answer me? All I said was hello," she insisted.

Marion shrugged. "Please, Marilyn, I don't know why. Sit down, please."

Still, Marilyn didn't move. She went to Brent, smiling. "What's the matter, Brent? Can't you talk or something?"

"Marilyn!" Marion corrected again.

Brent suddenly exploded. He jumped out of his seat and slapped Marilyn's face. She shrieked. He kicked his desk forward until it fell over. Quickly, Marion took hold of Marilyn and looked at Brent.

"We don't do that here," she said. "We don't hit anyone in this room. Now, apologize to Marilyn. Go on!"

Brent did not budge or attempt to apologize.

"Well?" Marion asked.

Clearly frustrated, the boy saw he was wrong but stubbornly refused to admit it. "No!" he exploded, throwing his books across the room.

"Goddamn it! Goddamn you to hell!" he shouted before he ran out of the room.

"Oh, dear," Marion sighed and threw up her hands. "Marilyn, wait here!" Marion hurried out and looked about frantically. She had no idea where he was. She heard soft weeping from an empty classroom and found him there.

Marion walked in, saying nothing. She carefully studied him. She wanted to reach out to him the way she did to Marilyn. She walked toward him. He sat at the back of the room at one of the desks. She found a chair and sat next to him. Knowing he hated physical contact, she didn't dare touch him.

"Brent?" she began softly.

No answer. He kept weeping, ignoring Marion.

"Brent?" she tried again.

"Go away!" Brent sobbed, not looking at her.

Neither said anything for a while. "What's wrong?" Marion asked finally.

Marion wasn't ready to give in. "Look Brent," she said. "I can't help you if you keep turning me away. Why don't you tell me what's wrong?"

"She hates me, doesn't she?" he quietly asked.

"Who?" Marion questioned.

"You know." He flushed from embarrassment.

She shook her head. "No, I honestly don't know. Why don't you tell me?"

"I can't." He sobbed. "I mean . . . Oh, I don't know."

He stopped crying and looked directly at Marion.

"What I'm trying to say is . . . well, you know. I can't bring myself to even say her name. I didn't mean to hit her, you know. It's just . . . well, I don't know. You know about me. I'm the only guy who never had a girlfriend. I have a father who . . ." His voice became petulant. Marion listened intently, saying nothing.

"How would you feel if everyone hated you?" he asked. "Wouldn't that bother you?"

"It would not, because if you like yourself, you should not care if others do not. If they dislike you, it is their problem, not yours." Marion replied carefully.

Then she asked, "Who do you think hates you?"

"Everyone, oh, I don't know." Finally, exasperated, he turned from Marion. "Do you hate me?"

"No," Marion replied. "I don't hate you." She smiled.

"Does she—you know, the girl in your class?"

"Marilyn?" Marion asked.

He became shy and blushed. "Does she hate me?"

"No," Marion replied. "Why should she?"

"I didn't mean to do what I did, you know," he confessed.

"I know." She nodded.

"I don't hate her, you know," he continued.

"I know you don't, Brent."

"She's pretty. She's nice, too, you know. She's sweet, but why does she yell all the time? It would be nice if she didn't," he remarked.

Marion said, "Yes, she is pretty."

"Why does she act the way she does?"

Marion shrugged, then softly replied, "Things bother her. She has problems. That's why she's here . . . like you."

"I'm sorry I hit her. I'd honestly like to ask her out." He looked curiously at Marion. "Do you understand?"

"Yes," Marion replied.

"Could you tell her for me?" he asked.

"I think you should tell her yourself. It would be nice," Marion encouraged.

"I can't. I want to, but I can't," he protested.

"'Where there's a will, there's a way,' I always say, Brent. You ask her. Even if she turns you down, the effort will show maturity—improvement."

"Really?" he looked up.

"Yes, really." Marion smiled at him.

"I'm sorry, you know. I really am. I like her, you know?"

"I understand." She nodded.

"You can touch me, if you want," he offered. Marion gently patted his back in a motherly way.

For the first time since she met him, Brent smiled . . . at Marion and to himself. The breakthrough happened. Brent opened up and started to show some feelings for somebody besides himself.

* * * * *

The first month was tough, but far from unsuccessful. Marion was a miracle worker, making progress with her two students. Nevertheless, at times Marilyn laughed at nothing or bit her hands or curled her hair while trying to work. She became restless, seemed to always move around, and was never able to sit in one place for a lengthy period of time. She started her work, then stopped it. She was always getting out of her seat, then sitting down, then standing up.

Brent openly complained about his father, who badgered him every five minutes for every little thing. The boy refused to work when he got agitated thinking about his father's nagging. Although no longer explosive, he screamed out obscenities when he didn't understand assignments.

Marilyn's learning problems also continued. She couldn't read or write satisfactorily even though she made an honest effort.

One day, after a mathematics test, she came into class grumpy. Her head was down, and she looked old and tired. She failed to acknowledge Marion's usual friendly greeting, so Marion knew something was wrong. Tears filled Marilyn's eyes. When Marion tried comforting her by stroking her wrist, Marilyn abruptly snatched her hand away.

"What's wrong, honey?" Marion asked.

There was no answer.

Slowly, Marilyn took out a test paper from her loose-leaf notebook and dejectedly showed it to Marion. Marion took it from her.

"I tried. I really did," Marilyn cried passionately.

"I know, darling. I understand," Marion said.

"What's the difference? She won't!" Marilyn shouted.

"Who?" Marion asked.

"Who do you think?" Marilyn snapped.

"Your mother?" Marion guessed.

That was the beginning. For the next two weeks, Marilyn came in upset and dejected. She failed a couple of more tests.

"Marilyn," Marion attempted. "I know you tried. I do, really. It's not you."

Marilyn was undaunted. "I'm failing. I know it's my own fault. Is my mother right? Don't I try hard enough?" She shook her head. "No, I know it isn't so. I do try, so it can't be my fault, but what can I do?" she cried.

In another week, the situation came to a head. Screams were heard throughout the school.

"Young lady!" Mrs. Simpson yelled at Marilyn, who screamed and threw her books around the room. The other students roared with laughter, shooting spitballs and calling her names. Marilyn couldn't stop banging against the wall, hitting it madly with her fists in a frenzy.

Finally, Erma Simpson wearily asked, above the commotion, "Does anyone know if Doctor Strauss is here yet?"

"Yes," a student spoke up. "She is."

"Get her immediately! Tell her it's an emergency!" the teacher shouted above Marilyn's screams.

When the student left, Erma said, "All right, everyone, ignore her and let's get back to work. Doctor Strauss will be here shortly."

* * * * *

"Marilyn," Marion asked when she arrived. "What's wrong?"

Marilyn would not stop. She hiccupped and screamed. Tears rolled down her cheeks. The other students watched.

Marion said, "I'm taking care of this. Please go on with your business. I can manage the situation."

The children turned and went back to work. Marion hugged Marilyn close and stroked her hair. "Marilyn, it's all right, honey. It's all right. Now, tell me what happened."

Marilyn's sobbing subsided. "Please, don't tell my mother," She begged, frightened. "Don't let them tell her, please."

"I won't. No one will. I promise I won't let anyone hurt you," Marion assured her calmly.

After a few minutes, Marilyn became calm. She didn't tell Marion what was wrong, although Marion questioned her about it.

"Let's go to the ladies' room and wash your face. Then we'll go to class, all right?" Marion suggested.

Marilyn nodded slowly.

"Why don't you get your books, and we'll go?"

Marilyn did, obediently. Marion looked at the teacher. "Everything's all right, Mrs. Simpson," Marion said. "I'm taking Marilyn downstairs."

* * * * *

Marilyn sat on a stool. Marion took a washcloth, wet it with icy water, and washed Marilyn's face gently, patting her eyes. She took a clean towel from the rack and dried her face.

"All right?" Marion smiled.

Marilyn still didn't answer. She turned from Marion.

"It's not twelve o'clock yet. Why don't we go to my room and talk? All right?"

Marilyn still didn't answer Marion. She got up and gathered her books. Both went upstairs quietly and calmly. Neither said a word.

When they reached the resource room, Marilyn took her regular seat at a desk near the window. She buried her head in her arms. Marion pulled up a chair and sat down next to her, then began stroking her back.

"Marilyn, I can't help you if you tune me out. You must tell me about what happened in Mrs. Simpson's room."

There was silence. Marion refused to back down. Marilyn would eventually tell her. She knew it.

Marilyn spoke with her head on her desk. "Mrs. Simpson gave us a test on equations. Everyone did well . . . except me."

She sobbed again. Marion patted her. "Don't cry, honey."

Marilyn lifted her head. She faced Marion, her voice rising. "I tried. I really did, but I failed. She told the whole class I failed. She held my test paper up and displayed it before the whole class. They laughed at me, called me names and everything."

She turned from Marion. "That wasn't right, Marilyn. It wasn't. What Mrs. Simpson did was uncalled for," Marion said. "Please, trust me. I'll take care of it."

"How?" Marilyn asked doubtfully.

Marion patted her arm. "Trust me, all right? Everything will be fine."

After school, Marion and Erma met in Mr. Marshall's office to discuss the episode. Although Erma didn't deny what she did, she wouldn't admit she was amiss for making fun of Marilyn. Erma, although she knew Marilyn's problems, claimed she only did what she did to make the girl try harder. She said Marilyn was bright but needed firm discipline. She accused her of being uncooperative and not trying hard enough.

Marion considered Erma an insensitive, callous woman. Because Erma had taught for more than forty years, she had to know about special children like Marilyn. She had all kinds of students. How could she be so heartless? Marion wondered.

Mr. Marshall didn't condone Erma's actions, but he didn't speak up in defense of Marilyn.

Marion had an idea she had never used for students with brain injuries. She decided to get a laptop and get technical help so Marilyn could have an account. Marilyn would be shown how to use it. But Marion needed permission from her teachers to help her student with her assignments.

The next day, Marion told Marilyn about her plan. The girl admitted she felt relieved. Marion couldn't see any sense in trying to teach Marilyn reading when she knew it would be as useless as teaching a paraplegic to walk.

Marion reasoned with Marilyn's teachers, and they understood Marilyn's problems. Even Erma Simpson relented.

However, the principal was reluctant.

To prove Marilyn could learn, Marion entered her assignments online. Marion showed Mr. Marshall her tests from the past couple of weeks. She hardly missed a question in any subject. Marilyn picked up the computer basics well and so quickly.

Mr. Marshall was finally convinced. He admitted he couldn't argue with Marion. Each assignment icon had a distinct color for each subject so Marilyn could do her assignments.

Marion won the battle.

CHAPTER SIX

"Is everything all right in school?" Joan Wentworth asked her daughter at the dinner table one night.

The house cleaner served each Wentworth family member. She ended with Joan, who dismissed her curtly. "Thank you, Dorothy. You may leave now."

"Yes, ma'am." She returned to the kitchen.

"Yes, Mama," the girl replied timidly, not looking at her mother.

Furious that Marilyn didn't raise her head, Joan grabbed her daughter's chin and pulled her face around.

"Look at me when I talk to you. Now, I'm asking you again. How is everything in school?"

"Fine." Her head didn't budge.

"Are you sure?" she demanded.

"Yes," Marilyn replied.

"You know, I'm putting a lot of money into that program to help you. If you're not trying, it's a waste of money—mine, that is. You know what will happen if you fail again, don't you?" Her piercing black eyes never left Marilyn's face.

"Yes, Mama," the girl turned away. Getting angrier, Joan got out of her chair.

She viciously slapped Marilyn's face. Marilyn hid, using her arms as a shield. Joan stood over her. "Look at me!" she screamed.

Gerald looked up from his plate and said calmly, "Joan, leave her alone."

Furiously, Joan glared at her husband. "You stay out of this! I'll do what I damned well please!"

Gerald frowned. "Joan, please . . ."

Still with fury, Joan threw a glass of wine at him. He ducked.

"There!" Joan smirked triumphantly. "Now, let me handle this!" She turned to her daughter, pointing a finger. "Go to your room, now!"

Marilyn left obediently, leaving her unfinished dinner on her plate.

Randall looked up from his plate, watching.

* * * * *

Later, after Marilyn went to bed, Joan quietly entered her room. She glanced through Marilyn's books, where she found a math test with a grade of 30% and an English quiz marked 20%. She looked through Marilyn's work—all of which appeared indecipherable.

An expression of horror crossed her face, contorted by rage. Marilyn was tossing and turning in her sleep. Joan dashed over to the bed and screamed, "Get out of that bed!"

Marilyn was terrified.

"Get up!" Joan screamed again.

When she saw Marilyn wasn't moving, she grabbed her daughter's hair furiously and yanked her off the bed. "Get over here!" Joan yelled. "Get up off that floor, now!"

Marilyn couldn't move, though she tried with significant effort. Joan got a back brush and started to beat her with it. "Bitch! Liar! Bastard!" she screamed at Marilyn.

"Please, Mama, please," the child begged.

"I'll teach you to lie to me!" Joan showed Marilyn the two test papers. "You're failing again, aren't you?" she demanded.

"No," Marilyn sobbed.

Joan ripped off the girl's nightgown from behind. She whipped her on her bare back with an extension cord. "Goofing off again, aren't you?" Joan continued to yell at Marilyn, hitting her repeatedly.

"Please, Mama. Please don't." Marilyn sobbed.

Finally, Joan put both the brush and cord down.

She continued staring angrily at her daughter through deep, dark eyes.

Gerald walked into Marilyn's room quietly. "What's going on?" he inquired.

Randall, rubbing his eyes and clad in his pajamas, stood transfixed.

Joan turned to her husband and impatiently handed him the two test papers. "See for yourself! Look!"

She dashed to Marilyn's desk and grabbed some assignments. He looked at them briefly, then gave them back. "So?" he remarked absentmindedly.

"So?" Joan yelled at her husband. "Is that all you can say? So, she's failing again, that's what. She's goofing off again." She pushed Marilyn's books on the floor as well, then threw Marilyn's handbag at her. The table lamp and clock went down with it, shattering on the floor.

"Joan, please," Gerald started. "Remember what the doctors said."

"Doctors!" Joan spat out disgustedly. "What do those quacks know? They want money, that's all. Well, it's wasted money when she doesn't try. She knows what will happen if she fails again." Hearing Marilyn's loud, uncontrollable weeping, Joan yelled, "Shut up!" She pulled the girl's hair again and smashed her daughter across the face as hard as she could.

"Joan, why don't you accept it? She has a brain injury," Gerald said.

"Brain injury? Bullshit!" she exclaimed. "She wants attention. Well, she'll get it all right." She picked up the cord again. Gerald stopped her, holding her arm back.

"Let go!" She tried to jerk away from him. "If she doesn't learn now, she never will."

"Joan." Gerald glared at his wife.

Furiously, she turned toward him. "What do you know? What do you care if she fails? You know what that means, don't you?"

"You can't accept her as she is, can you?" he asked.

"Accept her? For what?" she insisted.

"You expect her to be something she's not," he went on.

"Shit!" Joan exclaimed. "She's not trying. Well, listen to me, and listen well—if she fails this year, I'm putting her in a state hospital. Do you hear me? A hospital. Then maybe she'll learn you don't get something for nothing in this world. She wants to be babied, that's all. You think I don't know?"

"She wants your love, Joan. That's all she wants, and you've never given it. You yell at her and strike her, then you wonder why she's high-strung!"

Joan's face became contorted. "Don't give me that, Gerald Wentworth. Don't you dare try that line on me. I've worked hard all these years. If you think it's for nothing, well, you've got another guess coming."

"Oh, Joan, come off it. Your act isn't for Marilyn, and you know that. You worked for yourself—and your father," he added carefully.

"Don't you dare bring my father into this!" Joan retorted.

"Why? Because you love him so much? Because he was so great?" he taunted.

"He was . . . better than Mother, anyway. All she cared or thought about was her darling son. He was so smart, so educated." As she sneered at the memory, she had a flashback.

"My mother beat me, but I never cried. She beat me for things he did. She never beat Ferdinand. Never, no matter what. At least Daddy loved me best. He did," Joan affirmed.

"So that made him great? Being domineering, owning businesses, and acting like a bigshot?"

Joan was in a fury. No one had ever dared put her father down—no one, especially Gerald. She gave him a long, dirty look. She was her father's daughter. Everyone knew that, and he was king!

* * * * *

Rose, the Brookes' long-time house cleaner, silently served Brent and his parents supper, then returned to the kitchen. Clara Brookes asked delicately, "Brent, dear, how is school coming along?"

"Fine, Mother," he replied flatly. Not facing her, he was completely absorbed in eating.

Finally, Marvin looked up. "Look here, boy," he chided roughly. "Your mother asked you a question. The least you can do is give her the satisfaction of looking at her when you talk. Now, how is school coming along?"

Clara interjected, "Marvin, leave him alone!"

Marvin pointed his finger at his wife. "Now listen here, woman, I'm not going to have such impudence my house. Brent could stand a little beating for once. It will help teach him some manners."

"Marvin, please . . ." his wife implored.

"Look here, you, I'm the boss of this house. I don't like his attitude. I resent you babying him the way you do." He turned back to his son. "Listen here, boy, show some respect . . . and I mean it."

Brent slammed the fork down on his plate. He ran from the table, knocking over a chair on his way.

"Hey, you!" Marvin shouted. "Come back here, now!"

Clara interjected again, "Marvin, please, leave him alone!"

Marvin furiously turned toward his wife and shouted, "Now, look here, woman . . .!" He couldn't go on.

"Please, Marvin, leave him alone," Clara implored.

Marvin gave her a dirty look, then sat down and gobbled his food like an animal. "Shit!" he murmured angrily to himself. "Jesus Christ!"

Later that night, Brent was in his room studying physics and chemistry. Marvin walked in and watched his son, reading over his shoulder.

"You know, Brent," Marvin started, "You need to go out more. You spend too much time inside."

Brent didn't answer.

Marvin went on, disgust in his voice. "Seventeen years old and never had a date! You should be ashamed!"

Brent mumbled under his breath, not looking at his father.

"I bet you don't know what to do," his father mocked. "Isn't there some nice girl around? I could find you plenty."

Marvin continued tormenting Brent. Disgust turned into anger. Finally, Marvin pushed Brent's books off his desk with a shove, causing Brent to jump from his chair.

"Damn it!" Brent yelled.

Marvin grabbed him by his shoulders and wouldn't let the boy go.

"Don't you ever swear in this house . . . ever! Do you understand?"

Brent did not answer. He held his head down.

"Look at me!" his father demanded loudly.

Slowly, Brent raised his head.

"Fag!" Marvin mocked. "Seventeen years old and still a virgin. Seventeen years old!"

"Leave me alone, please," Brent begged.

"I'll leave you alone when you grow up, not before!" His father released his grip, turned and left the room, muttering, "Fag! Fag! Moron! Moron!"

Brent stood and stared. A scowl crossed his face.

A few minutes later, when Clara came into Brent's room, he paid no attention to her.

"Brent, dear," Clara began, "Your father honestly means well. He loves you; he really does. He just has trouble showing it."

Feeling old and weary and uncertain of what to do, Clara simply resigned herself to the situation and kept silent. She walked over to Brent, patted him gently on the back, then pecked him on the cheek. "Good night, dear."

Brent didn't speak.

She left with a mournful, pained look on her face. He returned to his books, saying nothing.

CHAPTER SEVEN

Marilyn seemed calmer after she was released from her reading assignments.

However, Marion noticed bruises on her face. Joan Wentworth put them there, Marion assumed. Marilyn wasn't as uncontrollable as she had been in the beginning, but something else bothered her. At times, she came to class dancing, skipping, singing, smiling, or laughing aloud. At other times, she went into stony, sulky silences and ignored both Marion and Brent.

Brent's work continued to be outstanding. His grades were always excellent. Rarely did he receive a mark below 95%, but when he did, he exploded, pushing his desk over and shouting obscenities. After an outburst, he remorsefully apologized and promised not to let it happen again, but it did—repeatedly.

Marion noted one positive sign. Brent started to relate well with Marilyn. Although he had resented her in the beginning, he started acknowledging her friendly greetings. Noticing the girl's learning disabilities, he read her books for her though he knew Marilyn had a laptop to do her classwork. He even tried teaching her to write better.

Marilyn acted at ease with Brent. She never criticized Brent's actions, but rather tried calming him when he exploded. She said gleefully, making a jerky motion with her hand, "Don't worry about getting one question wrong on a test. I don't learn so well myself. I know what it's like. You're smart. I wish I could get only one wrong answer on a test like you. You're a nice guy anyway."

Brent wanted to feel relieved when she spoke. All he could say as he smiled briefly was, "Thanks."

After working with Marilyn and Brent for two months, Marion decided to speak to their parents. She hoped to find out more about their behavior and home life.

Of course, Marion had no luck setting up a meeting with Joan nor with Marvin. She tried reasoning with them, to no avail. Joan was indignant. Marvin, as expected, was sardonic and proud. Both were responsible for their children's behavioral problems, so they refused to meet with her.

Marion settled on seeing Gerald and Clara.

* * * * *

Gerald came in on his day off, Wednesday at three o'clock. Marilyn was busy cleaning the room.

"Good afternoon, Mr. Wentworth," Marion extended her hand in a friendly gesture. Gerald took off his coat and handed it to her. She showed him a chair at the worktable, then took a chair facing him, as she said to Marilyn, "You may stop now."

Marilyn saw her father and briefly acknowledged his presence. "Is Mama coming to pick me up?"

"No," Gerald replied, "Go on. After we're finished, I'll take you home. Mama's working late tonight."

Marion said, "Get your coat. Please wait in the auditorium. Okay, honey?"

"Yes, Marion," Marilyn replied as she bid her good night.

Marion liked Gerald immediately. He was of medium height and weight with receding, thin light brown hair and hazel eyes, clad in a sports jacket with brown pants and a tan shirt opened on top with no tie. Around his neck was a gold pendant saying #1 Dad. He lived up to the records: quiet, passive, sweet, and understanding about his daughter's problems.

"I'm aware Marilyn has a learning problem. It showed up when she was five years old. The teacher said she had a problem, that she couldn't read the books. When my wife heard Marilyn was having problems, she denied it. And on top of everything, my wife had just lost her father suddenly. He had a stroke. She never got over it, for she was very close to him. She was her father's daughter. That was the only time I saw her cry. She never cried, not ever, even when her own mother would beat her, she never shed a tear. It was because she loved her father dearly. Thus, she refused to believe any doctor about Marilyn's problems, although we took her to doctors all over. Some were highly specialized in children's learning disorders, but Joan was too stubborn to believe it. She still is."

"Yet she loves Randall immensely. He has no learning problems. Joan is extremely affectionate to him and smothers him with love and attention like her mother did with her brother. Like mother, like daughter. Yet, Doctor, Marilyn is kind to her brother. She stayed by his crib when he was a baby, held his hand so he wouldn't fall, and watched over him while he slept in his carriage so no one would hurt him. She has never resented or been jealous of her brother. I have pictures of her kissing and cuddling with him when he was a little boy, bathing him in the tub, dressing him, and combing his hair. She used to color, play games, tell him stories, and sing to him. It was so adorable. She loves Randall despite everything."

Marion listened attentively. Gerald was shy and placid, but she knew what a devoted father he was to his daughter. He understood her.

"I know her problems. I accept them . . ." He stopped. He couldn't go on. "How's she doing otherwise?" he asked.

Marion thought before answering. She wanted to give him an honest answer, but she had to reply with some hope. "Mr. Wentworth," she began quietly. "I'm glad Marilyn's in my class. When she and I first met, she was . . . well, how should I put it? She was upset. Very much so. She told me she hated women—all women."

"She did?" Gerald asked quietly.

"Later in the day, I had a talk with her. I explained I didn't hate her and promised I'd try to help her. I got personal with her, telling her about me and my life. I happen to be a private person. That was when she opened up—started to relate to me. Still, she continues to complain, especially about her mother."

Gerald listened carefully, saying nothing.

"She tries to do well with both her learning and emotional difficulties. Emotionally, she's shown some signs of improvement. Now when she's angry, she refuses to talk. She sits and stares." Marion thought for a moment, then asked, "Mr. Wentworth, how is she at home?"

Gerald explained. "Well, most of the time she's quiet. She plays CDs mostly. When my wife starts in on her, she goes into a rage, throwing books and chairs. Once, she even broke her favorite doll."

"When she gets angry, Marilyn screams and sobs relentlessly. I'm ashamed of my wife. She doesn't try to understand Marilyn. She has beaten the child since she was five years old. I don't know what to do. I try to reason with Joan, but once her mind's made up, I might as well forget it. There's no stopping her."

Marion inquired. "Did your wife strike her recently?"

"Just the other night—with a brush and extension cord on her back. Her back's covered with bruises and scars. She failed two tests. Did you know that?" he asked.

"Yes," Marion nodded. "I also noticed marks on her face."

Gerald's pitiful story of Marilyn's life brought tears to Marion's eyes. How could Marilyn be anything but a behavioral problem with a mother like that? Marion continued to wonder what life was like for Marilyn, trying all those years, spending time in a place with not one sign of improvement. It made Marion sad—almost devastated.

Even though Marion knew of the abuse before Gerald came in, hearing it made her sick to her stomach. She couldn't comprehend such inhumanity to one's own child. Gerald seemed helpless.

"Another thing, Doctor," Gerald continued. "Marilyn frequently hugs and kisses her mother. She practically takes her neck off. She says, 'I love you, Mama.' I don't know why, after what that woman does to her. She never kisses me—just her mother. I don't know. I simply don't."

"My wife is kind to her two nieces—you know, her brother's daughters? Many years ago, when we went over there, Marilyn was playing with her cousins. Suddenly, we heard screaming. It was Marilyn, of course. I knew it was either Merrill or April who provoked Marilyn. They tormented her because she couldn't read and was older than they were. They acted cruelly to her, but Joan refused to believe it. She claimed she saw Marilyn hit one of the girls first, but I knew it wasn't so. I told her that. Of course, Marilyn tried as well, but when we got home, Joan whipped that girl brutally with a hairbrush. Marilyn screamed as loudly as she could . . ." He could not continue. He put his head down, shaking it sadly. When Gerald finished, another thought crossed his mind, which he had to mention to Marion.

"By the way, Dr. Strauss, the only time Marilyn is happy is when she spends time with my sister, Edna. Marilyn loves Edna and the feeling is mutual. She invites her to spend every summer vacation with her, and they do things together such as shop, eat out, cook, watch DVDs, and talk. One would think they were mother and daughter, though Edna has a daughter, but she is away at college or with friends most of the time, and Edna is bored and alone all day; thus, she is kind and loving to Marilyn. Thank God for her. She understands Marilyn perfectly. Marilyn even looks like my sister with her yellow hair, which she curls and pins back, and with her large dark eyes and curly lashes. They are carbon copies of each other."

Marion's mind raced. Marilyn loved her mother and would do anything to make her love and accept her. Still, Marilyn complained bitterly about her in the beginning. The girl never spoke about her father, who accepted and understood her problems. Marion couldn't figure it out. But Gerald was right. Edna was a gem.

"Look, Mr. Wentworth, perhaps we could work something out."

He shook his head. "I don't know. It's frustrating . . . day after day, year after year of repeated failures and beatings."

"Still," Marion stated, "I'm glad Marilyn is with me. She tries. She's reaching out more. I used to instruct students with brain injuries. Don't give up hope, please," she pleaded.

Gerald sat, listening.

"Marilyn's a bright girl. She's a whiz at math. She picks up facts quickly, shows significant effort, and is extremely eager to learn. She tries harder than some other children who can read and write. Also, her memory is excellent. When I quiz her orally about her lessons, she hardly misses a question. She learns so quickly she's able to do eighth and ninth grade work already. Please, be patient. Marilyn's doing fine. She relates well to a young boy I have in my class as well. So please, try to be patient."

Marion was as frightened as Gerald. She didn't know what she could do, but she knew something had to be done about Joan Wentworth. It couldn't go on like that.

* * * * *

The following week, Clara Brookes agreed to speak with Marion. She was small, slim, and mousy, but a sweet and pleasant woman. Marion liked Clara, who was quiet and understanding, although weak and helpless when it came to her son.

"How's my son doing?" she inquired tearfully and anxiously.

"Fine, Mrs. Brookes," Marion answered. "He's doing nicely in here. His work is outstanding."

"I know that, miss. It's not that. You know what I mean. How about his behavior?" she continued.

Marion began carefully. "He's high-strung and has a fierce need to achieve. He tends to get frustrated a lot. However, the last week or so, he has been calmer. He even allowed me to pat his back once. He relates well to a girl in my class who has a brain injury, and he helps her. At first, he ignored her or called her names. Mrs. Brookes, your son has potential. He admitted he would like to ask the girl out, and he's smiling more now."

Clara listened to Marion. "Marvin, my husband, constantly picks on the boy. I don't know . . . sometimes I feel so old. He's a physician you know, and he makes a good living. His colleagues look up to, admire, and respect him. We live well. However, with Brent, I don't know. All Brent does is read in his room. You say there's a girl in the class he likes?"

"Yes." Marion nodded.

"She has a brain injury," Clara wanted to make sure she heard Marion correctly.

"Yes," Marion acknowledged. "He helps her with her work. He's also trying to teach her to write better. I think he's doing well. We have a lot of work to do, of course, but I feel Brent can make it. I really think so."

Clara smiled. "I'm glad. I honestly am."

"Well, you should be. Brent is a gifted boy. If he could learn to control his temper better, he'd be all right. He shows promise, Mrs. Brookes."

Clara remarked, "I know, miss, you're right. I wish he'd open up more at home. All he does is read his books. Still, Doctor, I feel relieved when you say there's been progress."

Marion smiled. "Mrs. Brookes, it was a pleasure meeting you. I wish your husband would come up."

Clara sighed. "Oh, I don't know." She checked her watch. "I must go now. My husband will be waiting." Clara got up and extended her hand to Marion. "Nice to meet you."

Still smiling, Marion added, "I'm glad you came by. Have a good evening."

Clara left with a small smile of reassurance on her face.

CHAPTER EIGHT

"May I see you for a minute, Dr. Strauss?" Flora Burg motioned to Marion as she stood by her office door one mid-February morning. "It's important."

"Yes," Marion briskly entered Ms. Burg's office, wondering what it could be.

"Sit down." The order was cold.

When both women sat, Flora began, "Dr. Strauss, I have some news for you."

Marion could not tell by her tone of voice if it was good or unwelcome news. Flora was flat, dry, and unemotional. She did her job dutifully, like a programmed robot.

"You'll have a new student this afternoon. She'll study with Marilyn and Brent."

"Really?" Marion remarked, surprised.

"Now, Dr. Strauss," Flora continued, "this girl is different. What I mean is, she's not like Brent and Marilyn. She has emotional challenges, but unlike your present charges, she's a traumatized deaf-mute."

Marion listened carefully. "A deaf-mute? Why? How?"

"Who knows?" Flora shrugged as though she didn't care. "Her stepmother stabbed her father a few months ago. The girl saw the whole thing, so she was taken out of her school. They called us. When I told them about you and your resource class, they liked the idea. They didn't know what else to do with her. Your class was their last resort. There was no other place for her to go, except to a hospital for the mentally ill."

Marion listened to what Flora said about her new student.

"When will she start?" Marion asked.

"Her aunt, Ruth Summers, should be in around one o'clock with her. The girl's name is Katherine—Katie Van Buren," Flora stated apathetically. "God knows what you can do for her. Her teachers brought her books over so Katherine could do her work. I'll give you her file. You can read it now if you have time."

Flora went to her drawer, reached for the file, and handed it to Marion.

"If you'll excuse me," Flora said, "you can read it in here. I must go to an administration meeting now. They're waiting for me upstairs."

Marion asked, "May I take this file to my class?"

"Yes, I guess so." The reply was in Flora's uncaring style.

Marion went to her classroom. It was still early, so she glanced through Katie's file.

* * * * *

"Marilyn and Brent," she announced, "I've spoken to Ms. Burg. You'll be getting a new classmate starting this afternoon."

"Oh, really!" Marilyn was always excited about changes. Brent, who was usually uninterested, actually stopped working and looked up at Marion when she spoke.

"Now," Marion went on. "I want you two to make her feel welcome. You must understand something. Katie—that's her name—cannot speak. She can't hear, either. She's what doctors call a hysterical deaf-mute."

"What's that?" Marilyn asked.

"It's a psychological disorder, an illness of the mind. It's not physical," Marion explained. "She can read lips and use sign language, but she seldom uses those skills. Please be patient with Katie. Don't get upset when she won't communicate. That's what she's coming here for—to learn."

Marilyn asked, "Was she born deaf?"

"No," Marion replied. "A psychological disorder occurs when something extremely upsetting happens in a person's life. A few months ago, Katie witnessed her father getting stabbed by her stepmother. He was killed. Katie blocked out the whole morbid scene and became a deaf-mute. Our job is to be gentle with her while trying to help her get well. Okay?"

"Yes," Marilyn replied.

Marion turned to Brent. "Okay?" Brent nodded briefly, then he went over to Marilyn and saw her struggling with a difficult mathematics assignment.

"Do you want me to help you? I'm good in math."

Marilyn nodded. They went to work together, entering the problems on her laptop. Marion went back to her desk to plan her lessons.

* * * * *

"Dr. Strauss?" a voice called from the door a few minutes later.

Marion saw a tall, middle-aged, blonde-haired woman with large hazel eyes. Standing near her was a solemn, dark-haired, dark-eyed girl. Marion smiled.

"You must be Katie," Marion said sweetly. The child acknowledged nothing. Marion looked up at the woman. "You must be Katie's aunt."

"Yes," the woman replied brightly. "I'm Ruth Summers." She looked at her watch. "I have a meeting in uptown New York, so I must go. I'm sorry I can't stay longer."

"It's all right," Marion stated. "I hope you'll come in soon to talk."

Mrs. Summers continued to smile. "Of course, I'd love to."

Marion smiled back.

Ruth Summers gently bent to kiss her niece. "Good-bye Katie, honey," she signed. "I'll be back around three o'clock, okay? Don't worry."

She turned back to Marion with a look of despair. "Bye," she said soberly.

Katie signed "good-bye" to her aunt.

Marion smiled at Katie and led her to a seat. She looked at Katie and said, "My name's Marion. This will be your class in the afternoon. Your work assignments are on your desk."

Katie abruptly turned away from Marion and walked past Brent and Marilyn to her desk. She began her work diligently, taking no notice of anyone's presence.

Marilyn got up from her chair and headed in Katie's direction, trying to attract her attention.

"Hello, I'm Marilyn," she said gleefully. "What's shaking?"

Katie took no notice.

"Marilyn, sit down," Marion ordered firmly. "Remember what I said? Leave her alone, ok?"

Dejectedly, Marilyn nodded. She went back to her desk.

* * * * *

That evening, Marion read Katie's file. The teenager, like Marilyn, was a battered child. After she lost her mother, who died of diphtheria when she was only five years old, the aunt took care of Katie for three years—until her father's remarriage. Her father remarried when Katie was eight. Her stepmother was a prostitute. Katie's father didn't know of this until eight years later. He also didn't know about his daughter's scars and bruises, which were inflicted on her by his wife's relentless beatings. The woman was a compulsive liar as well as vicious.

At times, she tried to strangle the girl. She broke her arm, cut her head so badly it bled and needed stitches, and even tied her to her bed and beat her with a lamp cord. She did everything except kill her stepdaughter.

After the stepmother stabbed Katie's father, the girl screamed without stopping. The neighbors heard the commotion.

The aunt took Katie to her house and assumed full responsibility for the child's welfare. The aunt was rich and beautiful. She worked as a professional model and maintained modeling agencies around the country.

Though her own marriage had already deteriorated before the murder, she managed on her own. Supporting Katie was a responsibility she took to heart, especially since Katie lost her hearing and speech.

Marion glanced at handwritten notes for more information. When Katie was eight, her baby sister and she were in a serious automobile accident, which left Katie almost blind but, fortunately, she regained her sight a brief time later. Her sister was killed instantly.

Katie's father, a kind and devoted man, worked in a factory. He drank a lot and lost several jobs after his first wife's and then his daughter's deaths. He met his second wife at a bar, which she claimed she owned. She told him she loved him and would love being a mother to Katie.

They were married, then life was even worse for Katie and her father. He, like Gerald Wentworth, was totally at a loss when dealing with his wife's treatment of his daughter.

Katie's high school grades were always excellent. She did extremely well in English and French and was an honors student. She was a quiet child who presented no problems whatsoever, although she wasn't known to have had any close friends. She rarely socialized.

When she became ill, the school put her out. It wouldn't readmit her until she spoke and heard again. Ruth Summers took her niece to a psychiatrist, whom Katie still saw regularly. No change was evident.

Marion knew she had to learn sign language to understand her new student, so she purchased an inexpensive text on the subject, practiced when she could, and signed up for a night course.

Katie's behavior the first couple of weeks was routine. She went straight to her desk and did her work without noticing Marilyn, Brent, or Marion. Her work was above average. She rarely received less than a B in her courses.

Brent was aloof with her, but Marilyn kept trying to initiate a friendship.

Marion was at a loss. Even with sign language and speaking directly to Katie so the girl could read her lips, she still got no reaction from her.

As promised, Ruth Summers went up to the school to meet with Marion three weeks after Katie's arrival.

"How's she doing?" Mrs. Summers asked.

"She's a lovely girl. I'm glad Katie's in my class," Marion replied.

Marion didn't know what to say. There was no improvement. The girl did her work but ignored everything and everyone.

"Well?" Mrs. Summers urged.

"Look, Mrs. Summers," Marion began. "Katie's illness is psychosomatic, as you know. Such an illness can take a long time to cure. It has been only three weeks."

"No improvement?" Mrs. Summers said flatly and defeatedly. Thus, she turned her head to the side.

"Mrs. Summers, you must understand . . ."

"I love my niece very much. Why, I love her as if she were my own daughter. I've never had children of my own. Katie is my whole life," she emphasized.

"I'm sure you love Katie. I know that."

"Doctor," Mrs. Summers tried again. "If I love her, don't you think she'd respond or try to get well? I mean, I do love her. I want her to be like everyone else."

"Please understand, love can't always cure an illness. You must understand . . . I know these things. Trust me." Marion smiled reassuringly.

Mrs. Summers looked down. "Yes, I know." She studied her hands. "It's so difficult, you know. I try. I truly do."

Marion remarked, "I understand, but please don't give up hope."

"I know I shouldn't," Mrs. Summers admitted. "God knows, I've prayed and prayed . . ." She could not go on.

"Mrs. Summers," Marion cautioned, "remember one thing. I do, and it helps me tremendously. God loves you."

Mrs. Summers nodded briefly.

That ended their meeting.

* * * * *

Ruth went home that night to ponder over what Marion said. Marion was right. She tried to read the newspaper at the kitchen table but couldn't concentrate.

Katie went over to her and kissed her good night.

"Oh, Katie!" she sobbed as she held her. "Please, Katie, try to get well."

Katie released herself. Tears welled in her eyes, too. She signed, "I love you. Good night, Aunt Ruth."

She left Ruth watching her mournfully with tears in her eyes. "Damn," Ruth murmured.

Before Ruth got ready for bed, she knelt beside her bed and looked up. "Why, God, why? Why Katie? Hasn't she suffered enough? God, please, all I want is for her to speak . . . to hear. Please!"

Ruth whispered her pleas for improvement desperately, helplessly, begging to no avail. For what seemed the millionth time. Ruth cried herself to sleep that night.

CHAPTER NINE

"Brent's birthday is coming up in two weeks. I'd like to do something special for him," Marilyn announced to Marion as she hastily walked into her resource class earlier than scheduled one day in mid-March. She greeted her teacher with a smile, which Marion cordially reciprocated.

"That would be nice, dear," Marion said. Then, she shook her head sadly. "However, I don't think so."

"Why not?" Marilyn asked. "I think it would be fun."

"True, honey, but you know Brent. We must be careful. You understand, don't you?"

Marilyn continued pleading. "He's nice, you know, in his own way. He deserves something special, and I think we ought to throw him a party—a surprise party. He's getting better lately. He doesn't get angry as much as he used to."

Marion became weary. "Yes, Marilyn, that's true. He has improved, but . . ."

Marilyn cut her off. "I'm buying him a card on my own, plus one for all of us to sign. We could even have a cake and ice cream—a cake saying, 'Happy Birthday, Brent.' We could chip in and buy him a present."

"Marilyn," Marion corrected gently, stopping her with her hand, "that's thoughtful and kind, but a present would be too much."

Marilyn continued. "It doesn't have to be an expensive present—maybe one that costs about fifteen dollars."

Marion felt fatigued from trying to reason with Marilyn. She's right, Marion decided finally, but she asked Marilyn, "How would Brent react to all that attention and love? He's not used to such a fuss."

Marilyn argued. "That's the problem, Marion. He's entitled to some fun. It'll be good for him—like therapy."

Marion sighed heavily with dejection. "You're right, Marilyn. I admit it. It might help Brent. All right, honey, you win."

Marilyn jumped up and joyfully clapped her hands. "Oh, Marion, thank you. Thank you so much. He'll be so surprised!"

Brent innocently walked in and asked, "Who'll be so surprised? What's going on?"

Marion and Marilyn jumped when they saw him. "Oh, nothing," Marilyn coyly replied. She winked at Marion, then returned to her desk, smiling to herself and turning from Brent.

After class, Brent left quickly. He suspected nothing. When Katie got up, Marion went to her and said, "Katie, stay for a minute, please."

Katie signed back for the first time since she entered the class. "My aunt will be here soon."

"It's all right, Katie. This will only take a minute." She smiled.

Both girls paid attention as Marion explained. The three decided to each chip in five dollars to buy Brent a sporty tie. They reasoned since Brent loved ties so much and wore one to class every day, he'd appreciate another.

Marilyn wanted to buy a card, but Marion had to help her pick it out, since she couldn't read well enough to do it herself. Marion would pick up the cake.

"Won't he be surprised?" Marilyn gleefully exclaimed.

"Yes, dear," Marion agreed pleasantly.

Marilyn turned to Katie. "It'll be great, huh, Katie?"

Katie signed her agreement with a slight smile.

Marilyn acted excited. "Oh, everything is wonderful. Katie reacted twice in one day!"

"Yes, she did." Marion smiled.

Katie turned away without a smile. She collected her books, faced the door, and waited for her aunt.

"Hey, Katie!" Marilyn called. When Katie did not answer, Marilyn became upset. "Why won't she answer? She did before . . . twice, in fact. Won't she ever get better?"

Marion also felt disappointed. "I don't know, Marilyn, but she responded twice today. That's an improvement."

Marilyn said, "It doesn't seem like that to me. I mean, if she can respond, why doesn't she now?"

"I can't say, but she did show a sign of progress. That's what's important. Growth is a slow process. Katie will talk again, but it'll take time. That's all we need . . . time and patience. You understand, don't you?"

Marilyn shook her head sadly, reluctantly adding, "I—guess."

When both girls left, Marion felt pleased with the events. She loved those children. They were growing. That day proved it. She cared about them deeply. For they were a big part of her world.

CHAPTER TEN

What was going on? Brent thought endlessly to himself for days.

Two weeks later, there was much excitement in the resource room. Marion, Marilyn, and Katie arrived early to put up the decorations. Katie painted 'Happy Birthday, Brent' in big, bright red letters on a blue sign that hung on one side of the room. Marion had put an ice cream cake in the freezer earlier that morning.

The cake was put on the worktable so Brent would see it when he walked in. Brent's presents were placed next to it, with the two signed cards. Surprisingly, Marilyn intended to give him her own card and her own gift, as well. Marion was pleased when she found out. She felt Marilyn was growing up. She showed compassion for someone else, despite her own difficulties.

Marion checked her watch. The time was almost twelve o'clock. "Brent will be here soon," she said. "Marilyn, stand by the door and watch for him. When you see him coming, we'll hide. When he enters, we'll yell, 'Surprise!'"

"Here he is!" Marilyn exclaimed a few minutes later. "Here he comes." She ran to join Marion and Katie in the closet.

Brent entered the room, looked around, and saw the cake.

"Now!" Marion told Marilyn. Katie watched her lips.

"Surprise!" they called.

Brent turned his head. "Wh-h-h-a-a-t?" He acted dumbfounded.

"Happy Birthday!" Marion and Marilyn called in unison. Katie motioned with them.

Brent was flabbergasted. Marilyn went to him and said joyfully, "Open my present, please!"

Still Brent said nothing. His face clouded. "Why?" he demanded.

"Why what, dear?" Marion asked.

"You know . . . why?" he repeated.

Marion wondered what to say.

"What are you trying to do, make fun of me?" he demanded. "I don't need your pity."

Marion tried to explain. "This is a party for you. No one is pitying you."

"The cake, presents, this big card—all this is for me?" he asked.

"Open my present, Brent, please," Marilyn pleaded, overlooking his apparent annoyance.

Brent ignored her persistent plea. He angrily told Marilyn, "Especially you! Why would you even bother?"

Tears filled Marilyn's eyes, unfallen, gleaming like captive stars. "Why won't you open it, Brent, please?"

Brent pushed the gift away. It fell to the floor. Tears rolled down Marilyn's cheeks. Marion tried to console her, but she stomped to the other side of the room. She rested her head on her arm against the wall and wept uncontrollably. Brent continued to stand there with an angry gleam in his eyes.

"Brent, why are you doing this to us?" Marion asked him flatly, still stroking Marilyn's hair.

"Doing what?" he retorted angrily.

Marilyn sobbed bitterly. Katie stared, dry-eyed but upset. Marion didn't know what to say. Trying to reason with him, she attempted, "Brent, this party, the cards, the gifts, this ice cream cake—all this is for you."

"I don't get it," Brent said, irritated and confused.

"What don't you get?" Marion asked.

"Why she'd do it? Why she'd ever think of me? Why?" he demanded.

"Who? Marilyn?" Marion clarified.

"Yeah," he mumbled.

"She likes you. She cares about you," Marion explained.

"Really?" Brent asked. "Why would anyone care . . . about me, I mean?"

"You're special." Marion smiled.

"Me?"

"Yes," Marion stated. "You are. No one here pities you. Everybody here likes you."

Katie followed each speaker's lips. Suddenly, quietly, she walked to Brent and patted his back. She motioned toward him with a small, pleasant smile.

"What did she say?" Brent asked Marion.

Marion answered, "She wishes you a happy birthday."

Suddenly, Brent smiled. "I'm sorry. I really am."

"Open my present!" Marilyn implored again, walking toward Brent. She was dry-eyed and composed.

Brent picked the gift up and unwrapped it. He found a pair of cuff links with his initials—BFB. "Oh," he said. "Thank you."

Marilyn smiled at him as she wiped away her tears. "Happy Birthday, Brent. You're a nice boy. I like you."

"How did you know my middle initial?"

Marilyn smiled. "Marion told me." She looked at Marion, who smiled back. "What does the 'F' stand for?"

Brent blushed. He looked down.

"Please tell me," Marilyn pleaded. "Please."

"All right," he stated reluctantly, "but don't tell anybody else, okay?"

Marilyn nodded.

"It's Francis." He blushed.

Marilyn laughed, but Brent was not angry. He smiled slightly at Marilyn. Brent wasn't used to this pleasant, personal attention—or his feelings for Marilyn. She said she liked him. She said he was a nice boy. All that attention was new to him . . . kindness and love he found nowhere else, for no one had taught him how to relate to other people.

"Let's eat my cake now," Brent announced with a half-smile. "Before I get angry again."

"Look at the cards and present from us," Marion urged.

He read the cards. Marilyn's had a picture of a boy studying books at his desk with a globe and atlas. Brent attempted to read what she wrote.

Marilyn perked up. "It says, 'To a special boy on his birthday.' I picked it out especially for you." She grinned.

"Oh!" He smiled again. "Thank you."

Then he noticed a long, thin wrapped box. When he opened it, he found a tie in many different shades of blue, his favorite color.

"That was nice of you . . . all of you." He shyly turned to Marilyn. "Especially you."

Brent was surely surprised about his birthday party, especially the fact that it was Marilyn's idea. For once in a long while, Brent felt good about himself, but it was not to last.

* * * * *

When Brent got home, he heard a loud noise. To his amazement, it was not his father. It was his mother slamming doors and drawers, with Marvin begging at her heels.

"Clara," he pleaded, "what are you doing?"

"Don't talk to me," she yelled in his face, then turned to pack, her hands shaking furiously.

Marvin just stood helplessly.

Clara continued packing, then slammed the valise shut and faced her husband, her eyes big and bold afire.

"For once in your life, Marvin, just once, think about someone else for a change!"

Marvin stood transfixed. He wasn't used to seeing his wife angry. He knew not what to say.

Clara stood and stared.

"It's your son's birthday today and did you congratulate him? Get him a present? A card? No, you didn't, as usual. And he is graduating valedictorian of his class and got accepted to Harvard. And what do you do? Ruin everything with your selfishness. Brent loves you and wants you to love him, but all you care about are your meetings and putting him down all the time. Well, I'm sick of it," she grabbed the suitcase and rushed to the door. Before she left, she calmly stated, "I'll be with Emily. But don't try to contact me until you get help—professional help. I mean it! I've had it with you, Marvin Brookes. Up to here," she indicated with her hand above her head. "You're nothing but a manipulative, controlling bastard!" she screamed, in tears.

Marvin's eyes widened. This was not his wife. It was her clone. Then, he thought, Clara was right, but he couldn't bring himself to admit it. Clara slammed the door, leaving Marvin standing there helplessly, his head in his hands. Suddenly, the tears fell. For once in his life, he was defeated by his wife.

* * * * *

The days dragged on endlessly. He was alone and dejected. Rose just did her chores, saying nothing. Brent came and went. Neither spoke. It was not a happy situation.

Marvin was worn out. He refused to eat and couldn't sleep or think. But it was his own fault. He was starting to recognize his selfishness after all these years. He was a big man, over six feet, husky with broad shoulders, large expressive hazel eyes and thick, jet-black wavy hair. Yet, he did not feel so big. Not anymore.

"Let's face it, Brookes, you're a loser, even with all your brains. Clara is too good for you. She's right, you do need treatment, and if you don't get it, friend, you'll lose Clara and Brent, and then you'll be alone forever. You'll have nothing."

The telephone rang. Marvin sluggishly picked it up, expecting it to be a wrong number or a solicitor, but it wasn't. It was Clara.

"Clara?" he groggily said into the telephone.

She wasted no time with small talk and began: "Marvin, Emily—being a school counselor—recommended a psychologist whom she feels could help you. I told her you needed help."

"You were right, Clara, I do need help. I need you, Clara. I do. I'm all alone here."

"You should have thought about that before. Now, either you call and make an appointment, or I'm taking Brent and filing for divorce. I mean it, Marvin. I loved you and stood by you all these years, but as I said before, I've had it. You have a choice; see the doctor or it's over between us."

"All right," he admitted. "Give me his name and number." He reached for a pad and pencil.

CHAPTER ELEVEN

"Young lady!" Joan hollered. "You're insane! Look at what you're doing!"

Marilyn was undressing for bed in front of her bedroom window. Her shades had been inadvertently left up. Joan passed in the hallway, drying her hair with a towel. She glanced into Marilyn's room. When she saw her daughter undressing with the shades up, she dashed in, furiously grabbing Marilyn's arms. She pinned her to the bed. The girl wore only her white-lace full-length slip.

"I told you never to undress by the window with the shades up... never!"

Marilyn sobbed, trying to free herself from her mother's grip. She averted her eyes from Joan's angry glance. "Please, Mama!" she begged.

Joan refused to let her go. "Don't do that with your eyes! Don't ever roll your eyes away from me . . . ever!"

"Yes, Mama!" Marilyn cried.

"Do you want to kiss me good night?" Joan asked.

Without a reply, Marilyn wrapped her arms around her mother's neck and kissed her cheek.

"Good night, Mama, I love you," she sniffed.

Joan turned and left, saying nothing.

* * * * *

The next day was warm and sunny. Marilyn planned to walk to school that morning. Brent showed her the way once before, and although she couldn't read the street signs well, he taught her the directions from her home to school.

Marilyn put on her favorite red floral mini-dress and new white patent-leather shoes. She combed her hair into two long braids, which she bound around her head with hairpins. She reached for her laptop and supplies and pocketbook, then left her room and went through the kitchen to kiss her mother good-bye.

"Are you sure you'll be all right?" Joan inquired.

"Yes, Mama," Marilyn replied.

"Okay but come straight home after school. I'll be working late for I have a big deal I'm closing. It could mean a lot of money. Do you understand?"

"Yes, Mama. I love you," Marilyn told her.

* * * * *

Marilyn walked down Brook Boulevard. Some boys from her school were hanging around.

"Hey!" one boy called to his friends. "There's that crazy girl. She screams like a retarded idiot."

The other boys came to stare. "Wow! Look at those tits!" one exclaimed.

"Yeah," Frank, the first boy, acknowledged. He called to the others. "Hey, guys, let's do it . . . you know!" They made a circle. "Who'd believe her if she told?"

One of them turned when he saw Marilyn.

"Hey, look!" he called to the others, who also turned.

When they saw her, they hid behind some bushes a few feet from an alley. Marilyn walked toward the alley, unsuspecting and innocent. One boy walked out from the bushes toward her.

Marilyn stopped, then took another step away when another boy moved in front of her, also saying nothing. Marilyn stopped again. The boys formed a circle around her. She looked around, frightened, not knowing what to do. She tried to walk away, but they circled her in a corner with menacing gleams in their eyes.

One boy pushed her from behind, causing her to drop all her school supplies. As she started to pick them up, another boy kicked her between the legs.

Marilyn screeched, then Frank pulled out a knife. "If you scream, bitch," he threatened, "we'll kill you!"

She became terrified and didn't know what to do.

"If you tell," another boy said menacingly, "you'll get it."

Another boy pushed her, causing her to fall. Before she knew it, the boys were on top of her, kicking and hitting her at one time. They pulled up her dress. She tried to cover herself, but she couldn't. She wrestled to fight them off, but she wasn't strong enough.

"You're going to have the time of your life," one mocked. To his friends, he motioned with his hand and said, "Let's do it!"

They dragged Marilyn down the alley, although she still struggled unsuccessfully. They threw her down, then quickly unzipped and pulled down their pants with anticipation. Every one of them showed her their genital organs.

Marilyn was terrified. She had no idea what to do. She turned away from them, closing her eyes tightly, not wanting to see.

One boy mocked, "You like mine, don't you? Don't you think mine's nice and big?" He tried to force it, dripping, into her mouth. She gagged and coughed.

The other boys continued to taunt her, showing her their organs as well. "Here's mine. Look at it!"

"Mine's nicer."

The boys watched each other, trying to decide which one would do it first. Then, one boy said, "Let's all do it at the same time."

"No, please!" Marilyn begged repeatedly.

Her passionate sobbing drove them on. Finally, the five of them—all at once—tore off her dress, ripped off her slip, and pulled down her panties. They grabbed off her brassiere and began playing with her nipples, sucking and kissing them savagely.

The other five boys held her arms out and spread her legs apart, Frank put it inside of her!

Marilyn let out a scream. She felt her skin ripping apart. Quickly, one boy put his hand over her mouth. "You scream, you fuckin' bitch, and we'll kill you!" he threatened. He flashed a knife in front of her.

Frank looked at his friends. "Anyone else want to go?"

The boys stared. "No," they mumbled. "Let's go!" They picked up their books, staring back at her.

"That retarded bitch. She can't even read," one spat out.

They left her exposed in the alley. She didn't know what to do. She shrieked and moaned and couldn't move a muscle in her body.

Marilyn heard sounds. She felt terrified again. Were the boys coming back? she wondered.

* * * * *

Ruth Summers walked with Katie past the alley when she heard groans. She turned, but Katie did not.

"Katie," her aunt faced her. "I heard something. Someone may be hurt. We'd better go see."

They went down to the alley. A scream sounded, but it was not Ruth—it was Katie!

"Katie!" Mrs. Summers shouted excitedly. "Katie, you can talk! You can hear!" She cried out for joy, "Oh, thank you, God!" Her aunt put her arms around her and hugged and kissed her furiously and madly.

Katie held on to her aunt tightly, sobbing, "O-o-o-oh, Aunt Ruth! S-s-she's- h-h-hurt b-bad!"

A sudden flashback crossed Katie's mind. It was that one fateful night. Adelaide and her father were in the kitchen fighting. Katie awoke, rushed out of bed, and saw Adelaide picking up the knife. Katie screamed, "No!"

"I know, darling. We'll have to call somebody," Mrs. Summers agreed.

Katie freed herself from her aunt's arms. She ran from the alley as Ruth shouted, "Katie! Katie! Come back!"

The girl paid no attention but continued running toward the school.

"Katie! Please answer me!" Ruth called again.

Katie ran fast. She yelled in the halls of the school. Doors banged open and teachers came out, looking around, frightened.

Marion was preparing her lessons. She heard the screams but paid no attention at first. As the screams grew louder like a siren, Marion rushed out.

"Marilyn?" she called. No, it wasn't Marilyn. It was Katie! Katie!

"Katie, what's wrong?" Marion asked anxiously, not acknowledging the fact that Katie had regained her speech. She took her by the shoulders. Katie screamed and cried hysterically, unable to answer.

Marion's eyes never left Katie's face. She stood, holding her. "Katie, what happened? Please, tell me!"

"M-M-Marilyn," she stuttered, unable to go on.

"What about Marilyn? What happened?" Marion urged.

"S-S-She's h-h-hurt!" Katie stammered, sobbing. Tears ran down her face.

"Where is she?" Marion asked.

"On Brook Boulevard. My aunt is with her now," Katie calmly reported.

"We'll call the police. Stay here and tell Brent, okay?" Marion suggested as she turned to the teachers and assured them everything was all right. They whispered to each other and to themselves, then returned to their classrooms.

* * * * *

A crowd soon gathered on Brook Boulevard. The police and an ambulance were on their way.

Marion arrived, frightened, and knelt beside the nude Marilyn. She held her hand as she covered her with her sweater. "Oh, Marilyn," she sobbed bitterly. "What happened?"

Marilyn tried to tell her but choked on each word.

Marion said, "Mrs. Summers, I'll take care of her. You don't have to stay, but thanks."

Ruth slowly left, watching Marilyn struggle.

"We're taking her to Broadview Hospital," an EMT said. "We can't do anything more here."

Marion looked up at him. "I'd like to stay with her."

"Are you her mother?" he inquired.

"No, I'm her teacher," Marion admitted.

"We'll have to ask her mother to go. That's the rules."

Marion tried to explain. "Her mother's too cruel. She won't understand. She'll blame Marilyn and beat her to a bloody pulp. I understand my student. Her mother refuses to do so. Please, you must understand."

"Listen, lady," he went on sympathetically but firmly. "I don't make the rules. I just enforce them. If I don't, I could lose my job."

Marion felt helpless. She was determined to do something, but she didn't know what she could do.

"Let me call her mother then," Marion begged the EMT. Even with that, Marion wasn't sure she could help, but it was a chance.

Marion reached into her handbag for her cell phone and punched in Joan's business number at Astor Real Estate.

Joan sat at the head of a large table, conducting a meeting about the purchase of a mansion in Hyannis. A young receptionist walked up to Joan.

"Yes?" she looked up.

"Telephone, Mrs. Wentworth. It's a Dr. Strauss," the girl stated.

"Who?" Joan asked, annoyed.

"It's a teacher from your daughter's school. She said it's an emergency," the woman explained.

"All right," Joan said coolly to her receptionist. Turning toward the board, she said curtly, with an abrupt hand motion, "Excuse me."

"Yes, what is it?" Joan said angrily. "I'm involved in an important meeting."

"It's Marilyn. She was hurt badly, Mrs. Wentworth. You need to come right away," Marion said calmly.

Joan was furious. "Listen, that kid did nothing right since she was born. There's nothing like a good beating to set her straight."

Marion quietly interrupted. "Mrs. Wentworth, a beating won't help. Marilyn's lying naked on Brook Boulevard. The ambulance is there, but the EMT said only you can put her in the hospital—Broadview. Sign her in. Please, Mrs. Wentworth, she needs you. She loves you. I know she does."

Joan fumed. "Look, Doctor, that kid creates her own problems. She doesn't try in school. Then she gets hurt. Just last night she stood half nude by the window. Well, listen, Mrs. Bigshot Doctor, and you listen well. I worked hard all these years for that child, giving her everything. Put her in that hospital and let her stay there for all I care."

"Mrs. Wentworth," Marion tried again. "Please."

"All right," Joan stated reluctantly. "I'll be there."

She angrily slammed the telephone down. Marion jumped at the sound.

* * * * *

Marilyn lay on the hospital bed sobbing uncontrollably. She could not be quieted. Her voice echoed throughout the halls. Marion tried to soothe her by holding her hand and smoothing the hair from her face.

"It's all right, honey," Marion said quietly. "I'll take care of you."

Outside the room, a woman's loud, demanding voice resounded. Marion turned to see Joan Wentworth.

"Where is she?" Joan demanded arrogantly.

"Mrs. Wentworth, calm down!" the nurse at the desk spoke quietly but firmly. "Your daughter is in Room 103. First, a doctor will be out to talk to you about her."

"Why can't I see her?" Joan petulantly asked.

"Mrs. Wentworth, please, there are rules," the nurse explained gently. "Since her teacher had called 911 and was with her where she was sexually assaulted, she was allowed to be with your daughter. Also, Dr. Strauss mentioned how you abuse her mercilessly and fail to understand her challenges. You are not at all compassionate and loving to her special needs."

"Look, lady," Joan went on, ignoring the nurse. "I have a big real estate deal going on right now. It could involve a lot of money, and I was in the middle of an important meeting. I demand to see her."

"Mrs. Wentworth, please, have a seat," the nurse pleaded.

Joan continued her fury. "That does it!" She walked past the nurse haughtily.

"Mrs. Wentworth, it's against the rules . . ." the nurse explained.

Joan didn't acknowledge her. She defiantly walked into her daughter's room.

"Well, well, well!" Joan mocked. She burst into the room to see the girl lying on the bed with bruises covering her body.

Marion greeted Joan cordially. "Mrs. Wentworth, I'm Marion Strauss. We spoke on the telephone."

She extended her hand, which Joan ignored. She walked past her.

"What happened?" Joan demanded of her daughter.

"Mrs. Wentworth," Marion attempted. "Marilyn was sexually assaulted by a gang of boys. She's in deep pain and she's going to need your love, compassion, and understanding."

"What do you mean?" Joan asked sarcastically. "I worked my butt off for that kid all these years. Now she gets herself attacked. Well, lady, let me tell you something . . . that kid is going to an institution. First, I'll take her out of here. Then, I'm going to have her put away. Do you hear me? That's right, I'm putting that child away. She was nothing except a problem all her life. She doesn't try in school. She's babied by her father and by people like you. You think I don't know, don't you? I do. All that money, wasted all these years . . ." The woman turned to Marilyn. "Get up and get dressed! We're going home."

Marion interjected. "Mrs. Wentworth, you're wrong—completely wrong. It wouldn't be wise to take Marilyn out of here now. She needs to stay a few days for tests. After that, she'll be released."

"You goddamn mother fuckin' bitch!" Joan shouted at Marion. Everyone in the hospital heard her. "Don't you dare contradict me or tell me how to raise my kid! How dare you? Who do you think you are? Let me handle her."

To Marilyn, she reiterated angrily, "Get up. Get dressed, now! We're going home! Come on!"

Marion pleaded, "Please, Mrs. Wentworth . . . please!"

Joan ignored her. Marilyn struggled out of bed, trying to dress herself in the clothes the hospital gave her.

Joan took her home. Neither spoke on the way. When they reached home, Joan did nothing and said nothing.

Marilyn went straight to her room. She fell into a deep sleep in her clothes, not waking until the next morning.

CHAPTER TWELVE

"I bet it was that punk Frank O'Brien and his friends. I've seen them ogle her. Boy, I'd like to knock their heads off," Brent furiously told Marion when he found out a month after Marilyn's ordeal.

Marilyn said nothing about it for she was too frightened to do so. No one really knew who the boys were. Marilyn had an idea, but she remembered what they threatened to do if she told.

For days, Brent was upset, refusing to work. All he talked about was Marilyn.

"She's a beautiful, sweet girl," he told Marion one day confidentially. He was too embarrassed to tell anyone else about his feelings.

Katie, too, progressed after Marilyn's ordeal. She talked more. At first, she spoke only to Marion on a superficial basis. Later, she talked to Marilyn, and the two girls became friends. They talked on and on about their problems.

Marilyn mentioned that Katie's stepmother was like her own mother—a wicked woman. Both girls laughed and called the women names. Marilyn remarked that Katie's aunt was beautiful and blonde, like her birth mother was supposed to have been.

Katie loved her aunt dearly. Marilyn wished she had a mother like Ruth Summers. She knew how much Katie adored her aunt, just like she did her Aunt Edna. The girls exchanged telephone numbers one afternoon after school.

"Come to my house sometime, Marilyn," Katie invited.

"That'd be neat. We could listen to music. Do you like rock?"

"Sure," Katie smiled. "Who doesn't?"

Both laughed.

Brent still entered Marilyn's assignments on her laptop and helped her. He greeted Marion and the girls when they came to class and never left without saying 'Good night.'

One day Brent brought in a dismantled clock. He demonstrated it for Marilyn and Katie while explaining how each part worked. The girls weren't particularly interested, but they sat on each side of him and listened as he spoke in detail.

Another time, Brent brought in a camcorder. He demonstrated its use for the girls. They were fascinated, and Katie asked if she could try the device. Marilyn asked several questions on its use. Both told Brent how smart he was.

Brent also brought in back issues of magazines about computers and science he had collected. When he finished his regular work, he went through the magazines with Marilyn and Katie. He explained how various kinds of computers operated and what their purposes were. He devoured each magazine with such enthusiasm even Marion was baffled by his knowledge.

Marilyn remarked how much Brent was like her brother, as he too enjoyed figuring out how gadgets worked.

It was true. Brent knew more than his teachers. School was a waste of time for him. Each day he brought in a different magazine, a new theory, a new complicated formula, or a unique part of an electronic device. Marion was impressed. Katie and Marilyn tried to share Brent's interests, but they found such materials too complicated to understand. Still, the three acquired some knowledge about computers' practical uses.

Once Katie and Marilyn asked Brent to fix a DVD player.

"Sure," Brent said. He could do anything.

One time, Katie brought in her French text and tried to teach Marilyn and Brent the basics of the language. Brent didn't find languages fascinating. He only liked subjects dealing with numbers and formulas. However, Marilyn was interested. She soon developed an ear for the language. She and Katie started greeting each other and conversing in basic French.

Marilyn showed Katie and Brent photos and clips of her favorite musical groups. Again, such things didn't interest Brent, but he politely asked her about the kinds of music she enjoyed Brent admitted he enjoyed classical music, but not much.

The three became an inseparable trio. They shared their individual experiences with each other, trying to top each other to see who had the biggest problems.

They were three lost souls who found each other and couldn't manage elsewhere alone. Marion watched them interact with interest.

* * * * *

A few days later, Katie turned to Brent and Marilyn before Marion arrived. "Guess what?" she asked, smiling. "It's Marion's birthday next week . . . the eleventh. It's Wednesday."

"So?" Brent remarked without concern.

"I thought maybe we could do something special," Katie stated.

"That's fantastic!" Marilyn exclaimed. "What?"

"Let's surprise her with a card we'll all sign, and we can chip in for some beautiful wood flowers—you know, the scented artificial ones."

Marilyn nodded.

"What about you, Brent?" Katie checked.

"Okay, I guess." Brent shrugged.

"I'll buy the card," Marilyn volunteered.

"Fine," Katie said. "The flowers cost six dollars. I thought we could each chip in two dollars . . . okay?"

* * * * *

A week later, it was Marion's birthday.

The three students met in the hall a little before noon. Katie presented the flowers and card, and said, "Let's go in. Marion won't be here for a few minutes yet. She's meeting Ms. Burg downstairs. Let's put these on her desk, then hide near the stairs." They agreed and did what she suggested.

Marion went upstairs and walked into the classroom. She saw the card and flowers on her desk. She slowly opened the envelope and read the words. It was a large red card with flowers on it. Marilyn spent one dollar on it. It read, 'To a very special person on your birthday,' Marion smiled and put the card on her desk. She smelled the red roses. "Ah," she sighed pleasantly.

"Happy Birthday!"

Marion jumped and looked toward the door. There stood Marilyn, Katie, and Brent.

"Oh, thank you . . . thank you all!" Marion exclaimed happily. She went over and gave them each a hug and kiss.

Marilyn reciprocated. Katie smiled at Marion. Brent, as usual, showed no trace of emotion. However, he said dully, "Happy Birthday, Marion."

Marion smiled at them. She loved them.

Brent and Katie left at the end of the class. Marilyn stayed behind. Marion sat at her desk. Marilyn walked up to her quietly, shyly hiding something behind her back. She stood there, trying to get Marion's attention. Marion finally looked up.

"Yes, Marilyn?" she asked serenely.

"Close your eyes." Marilyn offered with a slight grimace. When Marion did so, Marilyn handed her a card and a small package.

"Open them!" Marilyn requested gleefully.

When Marion did, she said, "Oh!"

Marion opened the card. The large cardboard was decorated with pink flowers. There was a short, indecipherable note to Marion. Marilyn clearly tried to write on her own, with no one's help. As Marion read the greeting, which was signed, 'Your friend and student with much love always,' she smiled.

"Oh, Marilyn, it's lovely. Thank you." She hugged Marilyn.

"You won't tell the others, will you? I wanted to give you my own card and present, because as my note says, you're a nice lady. I love you." She smiled proudly.

Marion said, "No, I won't tell. Thank you so much," Marion's gift was a paperweight. "That was sweet of you." Marion embraced Marilyn.

"You do love me, don't you?" Marilyn asked. "You won't tell anyone about the gift, will you?"

"Yes, I do love you. No, we're friends. I respect you. I'd never gossip, so don't worry."

Marilyn smiled, then kissed Marion's cheek. Afterward, she put her laptop and supplies in her backpack and started to leave. She turned to face Marion. "Happy Birthday! I love you!"

Marion stood, smiling, as she watched Marilyn go out the door.

* * * * *

That night, Marion shared her day with Harold, who gave her an expensive 14K gold heart for her birthday. It read, 'To Marion, with all my love, HC.'

"Oh, darling, thank you." Marion hugged and kissed him.

They lay in bed, Marion in Harold's arms. He kissed her hair gently and listened to her discuss her day.

Out of nowhere, Marion said, "This was the best day of my life . . . next to the day we first met."

CHAPTER THIRTEEN

As the weeks passed, Marilyn's teachers and Marion noticed subtle changes in the girl. She ran to the restroom—at least five times a day. Also, she felt throbbing pains in her breasts. Most importantly, Marilyn complained about feeling more tired than usual.

One afternoon while going over Marilyn's geography work, Marion saw Marilyn gag briefly. She paid no attention at first, but Marilyn's geography disk slipped from her hands. She clutched her stomach tightly and coughed uncontrollably. Marion warmly put her arms around Marilyn and stroked her hair tenderly.

"What's wrong, honey?" she asked.

Marilyn continued gagging and struggling for breath. She couldn't answer right away. "I-I-I-I d-d-d-don't k-know," she replied.

"Is it your period?" Marion inquired, worried. When Marilyn didn't answer, Marion became fearful. "When was your last period?"

"I don't remember," she confessed.

"Was it more than a month ago?" Marion continued.

Marilyn hesitated. "Y-yes."

Marion jumped. She felt her panic rise. She continued stroking Marilyn's hair, her other arm around her. Marion patted her back gently. Marilyn was nauseated and couldn't stop coughing.

Marion turned to Brent. "Brent, could you please get water for Marilyn. I think that could help her feel better."

Brent smiled. "Sure, anything for her." He wanted to say Marilyn's name but couldn't.

Marilyn's head dropped on her desk. She was so weak.

She got up, with Marion holding her, and struggled to stand straight. Instead, she fell on the floor, her hands still clutching her stomach.

When Brent came back, Marion announced with panic in her voice, "Brent, Marilyn's sick. We must call a doctor right away. Go to the nurse and tell her. Please hurry."

Brent raced out the door. Marion still held Marilyn.

A few minutes later, the nurse and Brent hurried back into the classroom together.

"Doctor Strauss," the nurse said. "I called Emergency at Broadview. An ambulance will be here shortly."

"Thank you, but I hope they get here soon. Marilyn isn't feeling well," Marion stated. "She almost fainted."

"I want to go along," Brent insisted.

Marion was firm. "No, stay here, both of you."

"I want to know what's wrong, too," Katie wailed.

"I'll let you know. You two stay here and finish your assignments. I should be back in about two hours."

"I don't understand that particular problem," Katie suddenly pointed at her trigonometry text.

Marion felt tired and old. She held her hands over her face as though she was going to collapse from sheer exhaustion.

"Please, Katie, do the best you can. When I get back, I'll help you."

Brent started, "I want to be with her."

Marion threw her hands up in despair. "Brent, please. Please, don't drive me crazy. Do your work. I'll be back. I promise. Don't give me such a tough time. All right?"

Brent nodded dully, while Katie went back to her work.

* * * * *

Marilyn lay in Broadview on an examination table. Marion stayed with her, holding her hand tightly. Marilyn squeezed her hand as well. She felt secure.

The doctor entered. "Doctor Strauss, may I speak with you in the waiting room?"

He led her out, telling Marilyn to dress and wait.

When they were outside the room, the doctor said frankly, "Dr. Strauss, I have some disturbing news for you. Marilyn is pregnant."

Marion was horrified, but not surprised. She cried. "Oh, no! Oh, my God." She didn't know what to do. "As you know, Doctor," Marion finally said, trying to calm down, "Marilyn was here more than two months ago. A gang of boys sexually assaulted her. I prayed . . . oh, God, how I did. I prayed she wasn't pregnant. Now . . . and her mother . . ." She couldn't continue.

The doctor said, "I think we should call her parents and have them come in. They'll decide what to do. I'd suggest an abortion, but I personally cannot advise it without her parents' consent. It's the rules. Marilyn shouldn't have this baby. She's a disturbed child and having this baby would be wrong."

"I know, Doctor," Marion said, "but I think we should call her father first. He'll understand. Her mother won't. She never tried to understand Marilyn."

* * * * *

Joan was at a meeting that day, as usual. She attempted to resolve an important item in the contract about the mansion deal. A lot of money was at stake, and that day would decide the outcome.

Gerald was called at work.

"Mr. Wentworth," Marion said into the phone, "this is Marion Strauss, your daughter's resource teacher. I'm calling you from Broadview Hospital." She hesitated, then resumed. "Marilyn is pregnant," she said gently, "and rather ill."

Gerald remained his usual calm self. "I'll be there soon. I'll call my wife, but I must be frank. I'm terrified."

"I am, too," Marion admitted.

Joan was in a fury when Gerald arrived at her office. She screamed at him in front of everyone at the meeting. Gerald tried to calm her down, but it was futile, of course—as usual.

"Joan," he said gently, "please calm down." He put his hands on her shoulders, but she roughly pushed him away.

"Don't touch me. Don't you dare tell me to calm down," she said. "That does it! I'm calling the state institution as soon as we get home. That's it!"

"Joan, please," Gerald continued to soothe her. "Please."

Joan paid him no heed. "Today was the day we were supposed to settle the contract for that Hyannis mansion. It was going to mean money, and a lot of it. Now this! Well, that does it."

Joan faced her board. "Excuse us," she said harshly. "Tomorrow, I promise, that contract will be settled, believe me. You can bet your life on it." To her husband, she said, "Let's go!" She shoved him as she grabbed her handbag off her chair.

* * * * *

Screams sounded throughout the block. They were Marilyn's. The neighbors knew about Joan's abusiveness toward her daughter. For years, they were aware of her behavior, but everyone was afraid of Joan Wentworth. They all became victims. She was a tyrant. No one would get involved.

Randall came home from school. Hearing the commotion, he dropped his backpack and books on the dining room table and went into his sister's room. He was horror-stricken and said nothing as he stared, watching his mother beat Marilyn with a belt. Marilyn lay partially dressed in her slip, cowering on her bed.

"Get up," Joan yelled at Marilyn.

Marilyn didn't move.

"Joan, please," Gerald protested helplessly.

Joan ignored him. She continued to hit Marilyn, yelling at her to stand up.

Marilyn struggled to rise from her bed, so Joan put the belt down. "You led those boys on, didn't you?" Joan insisted arrogantly.

"No!" Marilyn sobbed.

Joan slapped her daughter's face hard. "Don't you dare lie to me! Do you think I don't know? First you fail in school, now this?" she said. "Get dressed . . . now! I'm taking you to Jackson State now. They'll know what to do with you there. I called them, and they're waiting. I can't handle you anymore."

"No!" Marilyn cried bitterly. "Please, Mama! Please! Don't put me away! This wasn't my fault . . . I swear it! T-t-they ganged up on me. T-they beat me. You saw the bruises. I-I didn't d-do a-anything," she protested.

Joan pointed a finger at Marilyn. "Don't you dare give me that line. The day before your so-called attack, you undressed right in front of the window with the shades up. Now, get up and get dressed, or I'll drag you by the hair!"

Tears streamed down Marilyn's face. She tried desperately to get her mother to understand. She screamed, "Please, Mama, don't!" She sobbed.

Joan said, "All right, you asked for it!" Joan put her hands around Marilyn's throat. Marilyn struggled to free herself from her mother's grip.

Gerald lost his usual gentle composure. "Joan!" he yelled. "Are you crazy?"

At that, Randall shrieked, his hands to his face. "Mother! Please don't hurt Marilyn! Please, stop!" Tears streamed down his face. Though he was his mother's favorite, he could no longer take Joan's abusiveness to Marilyn. He loved his sister but was powerless. Joan ignored both her husband's and son's attempts at stopping her, so Gerald finally grabbed Joan's arms and pinned them behind her back. He threw her on the floor next to Marilyn's bed. He slapped his wife viciously across the face. Randall watched, sobbing.

For once, Joan felt terrified of her husband. Gerald quietly pointed to her. "If you get up, Joan, I'll kill you with a knife. I swear to God, I will." He added calmly, but sternly, "I'm leaving you, Joan. I want a divorce. I mean it. I should have left you a long time ago. What's more important, I'm taking Marilyn and Randall with me."

Joan stared at her husband with a blank expression. She said nothing, staring as if she were in a coma. She was, at last, defeated.

With so much commotion, a neighbor called the police.

"Oh, Officer," the tiny woman pleaded into the telephone, "there's a child being beaten to death next door inside a house at the corner of Twelfth and Elm. Please hurry. Her mother is going to kill her. Please!"

The elderly woman refused to leave her name; however, the police quickly arrived.

The doorbell rang and Gerald called, "Who is it?"

"Police! Open up!" two stern voices replied from behind the front door.

Gerald went to open the door. He led in the two police officers.

"We've had a complaint from one of your neighbors," one began.

The other police officer said, "By the way, Mr. Wentworth, we also received a call a while ago from an Edna Sternhagen. She said she's your sister. Is that right?"

Gerald's eyebrows rose, "Yes, that's right, Officer. She told me she called you, but you were not able to do anything being she didn't witness the abuse clearly."

"That's true," he mentioned sadly. "We should have done something. However, we called her, and she'll be here shortly. She did mention your wife's abusiveness while your daughter was at her home a few weeks ago. She saw marks and bruises. She witnessed Marilyn having temper tantrums, outbursts, refusing to go out with people her age, being constantly afraid, shy, and sensitive of others. Your sister suspected it for years, but she really didn't know what to do. She was terrified of your wife."

"Oh?" Gerald remarked.

The first police officer continued. "Screams were heard." Gerald nodded solemnly.

"Am I correct, Mr. Wentworth? Do you deny it?" he asked.

"No," Gerald answered quietly. He felt the need to tell the story—the whole, ugly morbid, pitiful story. "It's my wife, sir."

"What's the problem?"

"She's responsible for it. You see, we have a fifteen-year-old daughter who has a brain injury. She was recently sexually assaulted and now we found out she's pregnant. My wife tried to kill her tonight. She tried to strangle her. I swear, Officer, that's the truth. She's beat our little girl relentlessly and mercilessly for ten years."

"I should have done something about her abuse sooner. I always thought she'd stop, or the problem would go away, but it didn't. It got worse, year after year. Everyone fears my wife. Her father left her his business, plus a large inheritance. Though she never got over his death, she thinks she's powerful and successful, like her late father, but that's over now. I'm divorcing Joan. As far as I'm concerned, she belongs in jail. She's responsible for Marilyn's problems. She ruined Marilyn's life—not to mention what she did to mine."

The doorbell rang again, unexpectedly. Marion came in and stared at the people.

Gerald turned to her. "Dr. Strauss, what are you doing here?"

"I had to come, especially when I saw the patrol cars outside. I was frightened. How's Marilyn? What's going on?"

The officer inquired, "Lady, who are you?"

"I'm Marilyn's teacher, Marion Strauss. What's going on?" she repeated. "Is Marilyn all right?"

"Doctor, a neighbor heard Marilyn screaming and called the police. She'll be okay, but my wife should've been put in prison a long time ago. She tried to choke Marilyn to death. She was going to commit her."

"Oh, my God." Marion gasped. "What will happen to Marilyn?"

"I'm divorcing Joan, so I'll be taking Marilyn and Randall with me. I'll sell this house and find an apartment. I don't want my wife near my children again—ever, especially Marilyn. Some people should never be parents. Unfortunately, my wife is one of those people."

At that, a car sped up the driveway, knocking over garbage pails and bicycles. Gerald turned and saw his sister getting out of her car in a frenzy, her hair and clothes disarrayed while slamming the car door behind her. She banged on the door of her brother's house, and seeing it wasn't locked, burst in angrily and out of breath.

Joan walked into the room, bleary-eyed. Her hair was disheveled, and her make-up smeared. "What's going on?" she asked.

Edna pointed at Joan, telling the officer, "She's the one. That's Joan Wentworth, my sister-in-law, I'm embarrassed to say. She beats Marilyn frequently. Look at the child's back. There's plenty of evidence."

Edna glared at Joan and wagged her finger sharply. "You should be put away for life. What is wrong with you? How could you treat your own child like that? Hanging is too good for you. You . . . you . . ."

Edna was out of breath and could not go on, yet she felt good. She spoke up to Joan and was no longer intimidated by her.

Edna turned to the officers, "I want her put away for life, and I'll see to it that it happens."

Still glaring at Joan with her finger pointed, she continued. "You can't threaten me or anyone else, Joan, not anymore."

Then, to the officers, she went on. "It's your fault, too, for doing nothing about it when I called, but at least you're here now and I know the problem will be taken care of. Thank God."

She stared with angry eyes at her brother's wife. She never liked her sister-in-law all these years, though she was civil to her. After knowing how badly she hurt Marilyn and made her afraid of her own shadow and of making a mistake, she hated her and wanted her dead. Edna wasn't one who hated anyone, not until she met Joan. There were times when Gerald and his family would visit Edna and her family, and Joan would speak harshly and criticize or grab Marilyn by the wrist and smack her in front of everyone for minor infractions. Not once did Edna notice Joan showing a trace of kindness to her daughter.

Joan interrupted furiously, yelling at Edna. "Listen here, you Goddamn bitch, you!"

"That's enough, Joan," Gerald said firmly.

"What's going on?" Joan demanded.

"You're under arrest, Mrs. Wentworth, for child abuse and the attempted murder of your daughter. Neighbors heard her screaming and phoned us. They were frightened. So was your sister-in-law. She told us how you treated her all these years."

The police officer took out his handcuffs and read Joan her rights.

"Both of your children will be taken away from you. We will definitely see to that. You will never see them again. Your husband wants sole custody of them."

Joan shrieked. "No! Not Randy! Not my baby! My little boy!"

Randall walked up to his mother. "No more, Mother. You'll never hurt my sister again. I hate you for what you did to Marilyn. I never want to see you again."

Joan cried out, "Randy! My darling little boy. How could you do this? I love you more than anything else in the world."

Randall stood watching his mother. He wasn't accustomed to seeing her in a vulnerable state, but at least he knew she was never going to harm Marilyn or anyone else again.

Trembling with fright, Joan tried to dart from the room, but the police were quick. One officer pulled her hands behind her back, while the other put the cuffs on her. Tears filled Joan's eyes and she sobbed bitterly, something she hadn't done since her father died.

She had a flashback. She was a little girl.

"Please, Mama, please don't hit me. I'll be good. I love you, Mama. Mama, why didn't you love me the way you loved Ferdinand? Why, Mama?" She paused for a second then cried out, "Daddy, Daddy, I love you. Please don't leave me here. Daddy, please!" Tears streamed down her face. Everyone watched, but no one paid her any heed.

The police led her out of the house. She stared at Marion. "I can't take it any longer."

Marion asked calmly but firmly, "Why, Mrs. Wentworth? Why?"

One officer escorted Joan out the door. Edna watched disgustedly and then turned away. The other officer remained inside.

"Sir, you'll have to come down for questioning later, and the juvenile authorities must be notified. Shall we check on the girl?"

They heard a loud moaning. Gerald stood transfixed, but Marion and Edna went in. The officer stood in the doorway. Marilyn lay on her bed—scars, bruises, and welts covering her body. Her face had a big, ugly scratch across it.

Marion and Edna, seeing Marilyn's tear-stained face and battered body, ran up to her. They both lovingly embraced the girl and held her in their arms, rocking her gently, trying to soothe her.

Marilyn sobbed uncontrollably, covering Marion's and her aunt's faces with kisses while they held her.

"Everything will be fine, I promise," Marion assured her.

"You know I love you, Marilyn," Edna soothed her.

The officer turned to Gerald, who had joined him in the hall. "It's obvious the girl is hurt. She'll have to see a doctor. It's the law. The welfare people also must be notified."

Gerald nodded.

Marilyn cried loudly, "Why didn't she love me? I tried to be good, so she'd love me. I did. I tried, but I couldn't. I couldn't get her to love me. I wanted her to love me. I really did."

Marilyn continued for about ten minutes, and both Marion and Edna continued to soothe her.

"Oh, Marilyn," Marion cried. "Everything will be all right. Come with us to the hospital now. I'll go with you. Your father will stay here with Randall. Tomorrow, you'll go back to school with Brent and Katie, all right? Now, go ahead and dress. Can you manage?"

Marilyn slowly nodded. Marion looked at Gerald. "Is that all right, Mr. Wentworth? Officer?"

Gerald nodded.

"Ma'am, if you're her teacher the welfare people will let you get involved in this, if you want. They're always short-staffed and you'll be easily approved for crisis intervention here." He glanced at the girl, then continued. "If you're agreeable, I'll go on then. Please don't forget to give the doctor my name and this case number."

Randall, perplexed and earnest, asked, "Will Marilyn be all right, Aunt Edna? I'm worried."

Edna turned and managed a smile to her nephew. "I know you are and that you love your sister. Yes, she'll be just fine." She patted his head. "You're a fine boy."

* * * * *

After a few hours at the hospital, Marilyn calmed down. She was given a tranquilizer that made her drowsy. Marion and Edna stayed with her.

"I know who did it," Marilyn said slowly and carefully, trembling as she spoke. "I do, but they'll kill me if I tell you. They know all about me . . . about my problems and that I'm a resource student. They know I can't read. They even know where I live. I'm scared, Marion. I'm afraid."

"Don't be, please. Don't be," Marion urged. "If you know, you must tell me who did this to you. They were trying to scare you, honey, but I can't help you if you don't tell me."

Marilyn slowly told Marion about every boy who was involved. She remembered every detail of the incident. Edna watched painfully.

"Why, Marion? Why, Aunt Edna? Why didn't my own mother love me? I loved her. I kissed her and tried to please her. Why couldn't I make her love me?" Marilyn asked earnestly.

"Marilyn," Marion said, "Your mother was a deeply disturbed and troubled woman. She shouldn't have been responsible for anyone . . . even herself. She couldn't deal with your problems because she never had love from her own mother. Some people never learn to show love. Your mother's like that. Nothing you did or didn't do could make any difference. She couldn't help herself. Do you understand?"

"Yes, I suppose. I feel sorry for her, in a way," Marilyn admitted.

Marion smiled proudly. "That's my girl. You'll be okay." She patted Marilyn's hand gently.

"I'd really like to rest now," Marilyn said, finally. "I'm tired, but I feel better. I really do. What will happen to me?" she asked.

"I spoke to your other teachers and told then what happened. They understood, dear. Your father will pick you up in the morning. He'll bring you to class, okay?"

Marilyn smiled and nodded.

Marion returned her smile. "All right, honey." She touched her arm gently. "Now, you rest. I'll see you tomorrow."

As Marion moved from the bed and headed out the door, Edna came up to Marilyn.

"By the way, honey," her aunt began with a smile. "Marjorie is coming home for the summer from college. Uncle Clark will have a barbecue, and since your sixteenth birthday is coming up, we'll all celebrate. All right?"

Marilyn's eyes lit up. A smile crossed her face. She was so happy suddenly and felt so good about everything that all she could say was, "I love you, Aunt Edna." She cried with tears of joy as she threw her arms around her aunt's neck.

After she released herself, Marilyn suggested, "I'd like to invite my friends, Brent and Katie, from school if that's all right. Marjorie has always been like a big sister to me, and I know she and Katie will hit it off. Also, since Randy is into science, he and Brent will get along great."

"Sure, darling," Edna approved pleasantly.

Edna then leaned over and kissed her niece and Marilyn hugged her again.

"I love you, sweetheart," she patted her hand and then left.

For the first time in a long while, Marilyn felt special and wonderful. She was loved and safe. She was no longer fearful of Joan's abuse. Never, ever again.

CHAPTER FOURTEEN

The news spread quickly around school the next day.

The story was in the paper, with Joan's picture on the front page of *The Star*. The headline read, 'Real Estate Agent Joan Wentworth Arrested for Attempted Murder.'

Marion knew Joan could hire expensive attorneys and stay out of state prison with an insanity plea. However, she was sure a court order would keep Joan away from Marilyn and that was all Marion cared about. Even without Gerald's and Edna's testimonies, there was enough evidence to convict Joan of child abuse.

Without Joan Wentworth's contributions, however, the school could not conduct special classes any longer. Marion wondered if that would end her program with the three young students. However, that was not her biggest concern at this time. She surmised, "I'll cross that bridge when I come to it."

Marion went to Sam Marshall's office to report the boys responsible for Marilyn's attack. She gave him their names, and Mr. Marshall sent for them.

"Frank O'Brien, Thomas Hicks . . ." He ran down the list.

He turned to Marion. "Dr. Strauss, I promise this will never happen again. I'm sorry it did. I'll take care of it."

"Those boys must be reported to the police," Marion said with disgust in her voice. Then Marion turned her head and saw the two police officers standing to her right, and she realized she spoke impulsively, for she was boiling angry. Feeling silly, she giggled to herself and apologized.

Mr. Marshall reassured her it was all right and that he understood completely.

Marion began, "Mr. Marshall, what they did to Marilyn was cruel and heartless. Those boys don't belong in this school. They need a program for delinquents."

"Yes, Doctor," he agreed. "I honestly didn't believe her—not completely. Now . . ."

Frank O'Brien and his friends walked in solemnly. They were hunched, heads held down.

"Sit down, all of you!" Mr. Marshall ordered. They slumped into their seats, not lifting their heads. Sam Marshall paced in front of them, stopping every so often and pointing at each one with great disgust. "You all know what you did, don't you? Sit up, Hicks! You, Haywood—look up. All of you sexually assaulted Miss Wentworth and she is pregnant."

No one said a word. The boys hung their heads in shame. They were caught and there was no way out. They wore shameful expressions on their faces and were unable to speak.

Marion felt strongly she would win. She knew it. They weren't going to get away with their crime, she would see to that.

"Why?" he asked angrily. "Why? What's wrong with you boys? Can't you stand up to someone as strong as you? Is that why you picked on someone so vulnerable? Do you realize you may have ruined that girl's life?" He paused. "Not only have you committed a crime, but she is pregnant. Are you prepared to pay child support for the rest of your life? What's more, how do you expect to afford that or anything else from a jail cell?"

The boys said nothing.

"Is this how you get your kicks? Well, your parents must be notified."

He glanced at the two officers and nodded. They took out handcuffs and put them on the boys.

Mr. Marshall continued as the officers headed to the door leading the boys out. "You'll all be put in Juvenile Hall, even prison. How long, only God knows. For my part, I hope it's for good. That will teach you to never do a thing like this again. What you did was serious." He looked at them coldly. "Maybe you'll understand what I mean after you see what they do to young boys in prison."

He turned toward Marion. "Doctor Strauss, I think we should close this matter. The boys will be expelled, of course."

"Fine, Mr. Marshall." She shook her head mournfully and said nothing as she stared at the boys.

* * * * *

"I'm glad Frank O'Brien and his whole gang are out of this school," Brent remarked in class one day. "They had a hell of a nerve. I knew they were the ones who hurt her. If they were still in this school, I'd kill them." To Marilyn, he said, "I mean it." He paused, and quietly said her name, "Marilyn."

Marilyn smiled at him, and his face lit up.

"Marilyn," he asked hesitantly and shyly, "would you like to go to a movie Saturday night?"

Marilyn's expression showed total shock.

"Well, Marilyn?" he asked again nervously.

Marion smiled. "Brent, perhaps you and Marilyn should wait until class is over to discuss this. We have much to do now. You understand, don't you?" she spoke cautiously.

"Yes, I guess so," Brent said reluctantly, with a slight smile.

* * * * *

The afternoon dragged on. Brent couldn't concentrate on his work.

Marion had all of Marilyn's assignments entered on her laptop and quizzed her orally. Her regular teachers, especially Erma Simpson under protest, remarked how well she learned her lessons. She couldn't read or write well, but she was considered brighter and more advanced than most of her classmates. She was already doing tenth grade work. The teachers couldn't keep up with her need to learn, she was moving so fast. She finished one assignment, then another.

Katie, as usual, did her work quietly. Since she could talk again, she became outgoing, though still shy.

* * * * *

Ruth Summers went up to school to check on Katie's progress. She told Marion that Katie made a couple of new friends at her own high school and began to show interest in boys—one in particular. The boy lived in their neighborhood and had gone to kindergarten with Katie. A few days ago, Katie recognized him at a dance. He never showed any interest in her until then.

Katie, like Brent, was upset about what happened to Marilyn. As time passed, Marilyn interested Katie the way Katie initially interested Marilyn. Katie's therapy with her psychiatrist also ended. She was going to be okay.

* * * * *

One day, after Brent and Marilyn left, Katie stayed to help Marion prepare lesson plans for the next day.

"Marion, I felt quite upset about Marilyn's ordeal. I felt badly. Then . . . her mother. Why did it happen, Marion?" Katie asked earnestly.

Marion couldn't answer right away. She considered Katie's question. Finally, she said, "I don't know, Katie. I can't say."

"Mothers are supposed to love their children. It's instinct, you know. Aunt Ruth said so. That's true, isn't it?"

"What?" Marion asked.

"You know that mothers love their children and only want the best for them?"

"Some mothers can't show love. Marilyn's mother was one," Marion explained.

"It's not right. I mean, that's why Marilyn was always anxious. She only wanted her mother's love. It's not right," Katie reiterated decisively.

"No, it isn't, Katie. A lot of things in this world aren't right," Marion admitted.

Katie continued. "I mean, Marilyn's a nice girl. Don't you think so?"

"Yes, she is. She's nice," Marion watched Katie.

"Her mother was cruel, demented. That's why she was the way she was."

"That's true," Marion stated.

"Aunt Ruth's been like a mother to me. She is so kind . . . so nice. Marilyn deserves to be loved, too," Katie emphasized.

"Yes," Marion agreed. "She does, but she wasn't as lucky as you. Of course, she has a father who loves her."

Katie continued. "I remember my real mother. Her name was Olivia Josephine. She had wavy red hair, dark brown sparkling eyes, and a glowing smile. She died when I was just a little girl. She was loving. It hurt a lot when she died. I watched her die. After that, Aunt Ruth took care of me and my sister, until she died, too. My father drank a lot until he remarried. Adelaide, my stepmother, was as cruel and heartless as Marilyn's mother. I guess we have that in common."

"I thank Aunt Ruth a lot, but I miss my father. Adelaide was harsh, but I learned something about her. She was mean because of her childhood—her parents abused her. They preferred another daughter and told her so. Adelaide used to say I reminded her of that sister, the sister she hated, the sister she resented deeply, her parents' favorite. She took her anger out on me. She was cruel. I did not condone her inhumane treatment of me, but instead of hating her, I pitied her for I understood her situation. I hope that some day she will get the help she desperately needs for her sake."

"You understand Marilyn's situation as well. You seem to identify with her, and that's good," Marion remarked.

"Marion, sometimes I feel old. I'm only sixteen, but sometimes I feel like I'm sixty. I've been through so much."

"I understand," Marion acknowledged.

"Also, about Brent. Sounds like his father was like Marilyn's mother, but I'm hopeful for him. I hope someday his father understands and accepts him. I'm right, aren't I, Marion?"

"Yes, Katie, you are . . . about Marilyn and Brent, and, of course, yourself, as well."

Katie smiled at Marion. "It's been wonderful being in your class. You're great, you know that?"

Marion smiled.

She was pleased. That was her world . . . Brent, Katie, and Marilyn. She succeeded with them. Their progress was slow, but it showed.

Harold shared her enthusiasm. Though his career as an architect was different from her work, he understood the brutal beauty of her work and her dedication to unwanted children.

CHAPTER FIFTEEN

"Did you have an enjoyable time, dear?" Clara asked when Brent arrived home around ten thirty p.m. the Saturday after he asked Marilyn out.

His parents waited up for him, pleased he was out on a date. Clara was doing needlepoint and Marvin was reading *The Wall Street Journal* in the living room.

"Yes, Mother," he answered. "The evening was great." He smiled.

His father remarked with a smile, "Son, I'm proud of you. I really am. You're showing maturity."

"I'm glad you feel that way, Dad. I enjoyed myself tonight. We went to the movies and saw *Summer Lovers*. Afterward, we went to Burger King for hamburgers, fries, and a chocolate shake."

"You know, son, I've been thinking lately. I was a bit harsh and hasty with you. I only did it for you. I care, but I was too overbearing. I hope you understand," Marvin said, struggling with his words.

"Your mother was right. I was a controlling son-of-a-gun. I'm glad I went to the psychologist Aunt Emily recommended. She really helped me. You see, son, all during my childhood years my own father put me down constantly. He didn't believe in praise or showing love. He felt it was just for sissies. It made him feel like a man putting me down for being a doctor. Never once did he congratulate me. Not once. I'm sorry. I only did what I was taught to by my father. I realize now that was wrong. The doctor is really helping me come to terms with my problems in being a good parent to you."

Clara looked up from her needlepoint, smiled at her husband, and reached for his hand.

"I'm feeling better about myself," Brent admitted.

Marvin smiled. "That's my boy. I'm proud of you. I want you to know I always was proud, even when I didn't show it."

"I know, Dad." He looked at his mother for a moment, then turned to his father. "Perhaps we could go to a ballgame someday, just you and me?"

"Yes, I'd like that, son."

"Well, good night, Mom, Dad." Brent kissed his mother. After Brent went upstairs, Clara turned to her husband. "Oh, Marvin, I knew someday you'd let us see you're human. I knew it. I'm so proud." She moved closer to him.

"Yes, dear. I guess I'm beginning to mellow." He put his newspaper down and did something else he hadn't done in a long time—he reached for his wife's hand and kissed it.

Clara smiled and laughed lightly. "Why, Marvin."

"Let's go upstairs and turn on that comedy show you enjoy so much. I may even like it, who knows?" He smiled at her.

Together, they went upstairs.

"Oh, Marvin, I knew there was a positive side to you. I knew it. Deep down, I knew it." Marvin kissed his wife's cheek and slowly embraced her. They exchanged a long, tender kiss at the top of the stairs.

"I love you, Clara. I always did, but I had some trouble showing it. You understand, don't you?"

"Yes, dear. Yes."

Clara laughed as she threw her head back.

Quickly, Marvin grasped his wife's hand. While laughing, they raced to their bedroom and Marvin flipped on the television. Both jumped on the bed giggling hysterically at the program. Marvin was laughing as Clara playfully tapped him on the behind.

CHAPTER SIXTEEN

What was to be?

It was June, a time for changes, a time for decisions.

Gerald Wentworth sold his house and Joan's business. He made a handsome profit. The divorce did not take as long as Gerald expected. He signed the papers, and it was final as far as he was concerned.

He and Marilyn were spared a great deal of pain when the boys confessed to the sexual assault and Joan's attorney advised her not to deny the abuse. Although none of them were sent to the state prison, the boys were put into a juvenile facility and Joan was committed to a hospital for the criminally insane. Even Randall refused to see his mother again.

As soon as their court appearances were done, Gerald, Marilyn, and Randall tried to put the past behind them and look to the future.

Gerald and his children moved into a small, homey apartment. Without Joan, he couldn't afford Dorothy, their long-time, loyal housekeeper, so Gerald had to regretfully let her go, agreeing to give her a letter of recommendation. Edna volunteered to come over and help with the cooking and other domestic responsibilities, as well. She also took Marilyn to a woman's clinic for an abortion, which she decided was the best solution.

Marilyn dealt with the events better than Marion expected. She showed significant improvement, and she selected a private psychotherapist to help her overcome her psychological scars.

Marilyn and Katie continued their friendship with phone calls and visits. The girls experimented with make-up and fashion. They rode bikes and jogged together.

Most of Marilyn's annoying, immature habits disappeared. She no longer laughed inappropriately. She kept her composure when she felt tense. She no longer needed physical comfort from Marion.

Marilyn's teachers, Erma Simpson in particular, remarked about her improvements. She had no more turbulent incidents with her classmates, and she related better to them. She even went to popular spots after school with friends.

Marilyn's assignments and examinations would be put online so she would have easy access to her classwork. Her teachers did not mind since Marilyn made so much progress. Soon she was ready to go to a regular high school like everybody else, with all her schoolwork on her laptop.

* * * * *

Brent, too, showed promise. He was still testy, but he was aware of his temper and was able to stop himself before he got violent and out of control.

After his first date, Brent told Marion about what happened. "I'm going to go out again."

Another change in Brent came because of his father's behavior. He mentioned in class, "I spoke to my father Saturday night for the first time in a long time. He listened. He really did," Brent added proudly. "We talked. I told him about Marilyn, that I like her a lot. She's wonderful. She's great, but I don't know if I love her. Maybe . . ." He couldn't continue. "That's not important," he said. "Not now, anyway." He smiled.

Clara spoke to Marion. "I'm happy, Doctor. Brent and his father are getting along fine now. I'm glad. Marvin is starting to mellow. He tries to understand Brent's problems. It was at my insistence that he go for help, and he did. It wasn't easy, but he's doing it."

"Also, I'm going back to work at the nursery school I directed before I got married. It happened that the former director just recently retired, and they needed someone immediately. Thus, they called me. Marvin seemed pleased. Anyway, I'm doing it." Clara sighed pleasantly with a smile.

Marion then said, "Good for you, Mrs. Brookes, and the best of luck."

Clara touched Marion's hand slightly. "Thank you, Doctor. He can go back to his regular school."

Brent's therapy was terminated because of his progress. Brent was due to graduate in June. He planned to attend Harvard to study mathematics and become a statistician.

Marvin went up to the school to meet Marion. "I feel so good—so proud, Doctor," he began. "Brent's improving. So am I. I had some problems with him before. I felt threatened having a genius for a son. I was jealous trying to be a hotshot. The therapist my sister-in-law recommended said I was repeating the way my father raised me. It was all I knew, and I was wrong, Doctor. Well, that's over now. I'm proud of Brent and myself, too."

Marion smiled at him. "Yes, Dr. Brookes. You're right. Brent is a fine boy. He will succeed."

He stood and shook hands with Marion. "Thank you, Dr. Strauss. You taught Brent well."

* * * * *

Katie, too, was going back to her regular high school and was in her senior year. She dated a young boy named Michael O'Reilly. Katie told Marion, Marilyn, and Brent about him.

"He's terrific," she announced gleefully after their first date. She was excited. "He really is. He never even noticed me before. He's not that handsome, but he's—you know—cute, with dimples. He's about five feet five, has blonde hair, and freckles. He's not much of a student, but that's okay. I mean, it's all right. He likes me. That's all that's important."

They were all happy for her.

* * * * *

Finally, the last day arrived. There were parties throughout the school. No one worked. Marion stayed in the resource room at her desk.

Marilyn stayed in her regular homeroom, celebrating the end of the year.

Brent went to his own high school graduation ceremony, where he graduated with highest honors.

Katie stayed at her regular school to pick up her report card. She made the Honor Roll with an A average.

They planned to see Marion later in the day.

Tears came to Marion's eyes. She thought about them . . . her children. She loved them as if they were her own. She knew she'd never see them again. She knew that day was the end. However, she didn't know they planned to come in to say good-bye with a surprise.

Marion glanced at her watch. It was close to two o'clock, but there was no sign of them. Harold was due to pick her up. He had something important to ask her, but she didn't know what it was.

"Hey!" a voice called from the doorway. Marion saw Harold wave for her to go to him.

"Hi, darling!" he greeted her.

She went up to him. They kissed. Then Marion turned away, trying to hide an escaped tear. Still holding her, he asked, "What's wrong?"

Marion shook her head quickly.

"Nothing . . . nothing, really."

Harold wasn't dissuaded. He knew Marion long enough to know when something was wrong.

"I don't believe you," he said. "I know something is wrong."

"Oh, Harold!" She sobbed helplessly as he held her. He gently patted her back.

"What's wrong? Please tell me," he pleaded.

"O-o-oh I don't know," Marion shrugged.

"It's those kids, isn't it?" Harold asked. "Well, look, you did an excellent job, and . . ."

Marion cut him off softly. "Yes, but I-I-I . . ." She didn't go on. At the door stood Marilyn, Katie, and Brent. Marion's face opened with a surprised smile. She felt relieved and glad.

"You thought we wouldn't come?" Brent asked with a mischievous, little-boy grin.

"Surprise! Surprise!" Katie giggled.

Marilyn held a large package and smiled. She handed it to Marion.

"Oh!" Marion exclaimed. She cried tears of joy.

"Don't cry, Marion, honey," Harold said gently. "They're here. You should be glad."

"I am . . . I am," Marion said sincerely. "I'm so happy."

She opened the present—a beauty set including cologne, powder, and bubble bath beads.

"Oh!" she exclaimed. "Oh, thank you. Thank you all!"

She kissed and hugged each one of them. Brent even allowed himself to be touched. He didn't pull away. Marion was so impressed with the trio, she forgot about Harold. When she glanced at him, she said, "Oh, I almost forgot. Please forgive me, Harold. These are the children I told you about . . . Brent, Marilyn, and Katie."

Harold smiled at them. "Hello. Marion told me all about you."

Brent was interested. "Who are you—a friend of Marion's?"

Harold blushed and smiled. "Why, yes, I guess you can say I am."

"Really?" Katie remarked shyly.

Marion smiled "A good friend, you might say."

"More than a good friend," Harold added.

"Harold!" Marion exclaimed. "Please, I think certain things are too personal to bring up here."

"I don't think the fact that I'm going to marry you needs to be kept a secret," Harold said.

Marion was stunned. "Harold, really. . . I-I-I . . ." Harold reached into his pocket. He drew out a small box and opened it. It contained a beautiful diamond engagement ring. Marion was astonished. "It's beautiful, but . . . I . . ."

"No buts about it," he stated firmly. "I want you for my wife, Marion. That's that!" He slipped the ring on her finger and gently kissed her hand.

Marion didn't say anything. She couldn't speak.

"Marry him!" the three children shouted joyously. "Marry him!"

Harold looked at them, then at Marion. She laughed. "Oh, all right," she agreed, "but when? I've got plans to make, you know."

"Yes, I know," Harold affirmed. "First, I think we should go out for a late brunch." He checked his watch. "It's almost three o'clock. I think now would be a suitable time to leave."

Marion nodded to Harold, then turned toward her children, the ones she'd never had, the ones she'd never have again.

"Yes, Harold." She softly shrugged and looked at them. "Well, I guess this is it, troop."

Tears filled their eyes. Marilyn showed her a small card. 'To our friend, Marion, with love. You stand for beauty in a tough, brutal world. Thank you for you.' Marilyn, Katie, and Brent signed it.

"Oh, thank you so much!" Marion cried.

"We'll never forget you," Brent promised.

"Never," Katie and Marilyn agreed in unison.

"I know," Marion said.

"It's time to go now," Harold told Marion.

"Yes," Marion agreed reluctantly. To the students, with a smile she said, "Good-bye."

Marilyn kissed her cheek. Marion reciprocated. Katie gave her a quick peck. Brent shyly said, "Good-bye." He kissed her cheek. "Good luck, Marion." He even shook Harold's hand and wished them luck.

It was over. The three children left. Going out the door, they turned to wave at Marion and Harold.

"We love you!" they called finally. "We'll always remember you!"

Marion and Harold watched the youngsters go. "Bye, now. I love you!" Marion called.

EPILOGUE

Marion and Harold married six months later and went to China for their honeymoon. Marion found a new position teaching children with brain injuries and emotional challenges in uptown New York City. Harold started his own architectural business and taught architecture at a local college.

Marilyn graduated from high school. She never learned to read much, but she did exceptionally well and made a couple of friends at her school. She had an A average, made the Arista society, and participated in a dance and music club. Later, she worked part-time as a model for a small company.

Brent studied mathematics at Harvard and did well. He made the Dean's List and was chosen President of the Alpha Beta Society.

Katie graduated from high school with a B+ average. She worked as an office manager in a dress firm and became engaged to Michael.

ARLENE AND RUBIN: A LOVE STORY

PART ONE
ARLENE

CHAPTER ONE

They frolicked around on the bed one cool evening in mid-October and giggled. He kissed her breasts, and she massaged his back.

"I love you, Juliajo," he whispered. "I love you so." He got hard and put it in her gently.

She cried, "Oh," her mouth on his.

"I love you," he said again.

Juliajo looked at the clock near the bed, her white full-length slip barely covering her breasts, reaching down to her knees. He ignored her while petting her between the legs, still hard.

"It's time to go now," she said quietly. "I have to go to work tomorrow."

He continued kissing her and whispered, "Oh, how I love you so."

"I must get some sleep. Much as I hate this night to end, I have work tomorrow," she insisted.

Finally, Spencer relented. He sat up and put on his trousers, then his shirt and buttoned it up.

"I love you, Juliajo," he said.

She looked at him, a question in her eyes.

"Would you marry me?"

With a smile, he replied, "Yeah, sure, if you were pregnant."

"Really?" she asked.

"Yes," he said. "I love you." He kissed her good night. "Bye, darlin'."

* * * * *

Juliajo and Spencer had met six months before, at the dollar store where Juliajo worked as a clerk. He came in one day in early April as she was putting price tags on some sweaters.

He had come in just to browse and saw her from behind—her wavy, thick blonde hair with strands falling down her back. She turned for a second, then she saw him.

He was tall, about six feet, rugged, and with cute dimples on his cheeks. She liked his smile. He loved her large, deep brown eyes that shone when she smiled. He told her he owned a bar on the next block. She was seventeen and he was twenty-three years old.

That had been the beginning.

* * * * *

"You have six months, Miss Gilbert," the doctor announced.

A smile crossed Juliajo's face as she began dressing.

"A baby! I'm going to have a baby!" she exclaimed "Oh, I just can't wait 'til tonight when I tell him. We're going to a show tonight. Afterward, I'll tell him—then we'll get married. Oh," she said, "Spencer will be so happy! Our baby!"

The doctor heard her but said nothing as he put his stethoscope away.

"Good luck," he said at last.

* * * * *

Juliajo looked at her watch that night. It was eight p.m. 'Where is he?' she asked herself. She was wearing a low-cut black dress with a red rose pinned on one strap. She was concerned. He was supposed to pick her up at seven. What could have happened?

She paced up and down in the hallway. Soon it was eight thirty. She did not understand. He was always punctual.

She sat down. It was nine p.m. and he still hadn't shown up. Perhaps he got sick or his car broke down, she reasoned. She decided to call him.

When she reached him, she heard the clinking of glasses, the laughter of women, and music blaring in the background.

"Spencer?" she asked.

He did not answer.

"You were supposed to pick me up at seven. We were going to see that show, don't you remember?"

Spencer still did not answer. She could hear his chuckle as he hung up on her.

She did not know what to do. 'What's happening?' she wondered. 'What's going on?' She decided to go to his apartment. She would get an explanation.

In her car, she feared the worst.

When she got there, she heard loud noises and the voices of women coming from Spencer's apartment. She rang the bell.

Spencer opened it. With him was an insipid short blonde woman, leaning on him as he smiled at her. "Later, okay, honey?"

"Sure, sugarplum," the girl said coyly.

Juliajo couldn't believe her eyes.

Spencer's face clouded when he saw her. "What is it?" he asked.

Juliajo was stunned. Tears filled her eyes.

"I'm pregnant," she announced, observing all the women in the living room.

He laughed aloud so everyone could hear. "Ha! Who's the father?"

Her tears streamed down her face. She stuttered. "Y-you said if I was pregnant, you'd marry me."

He laughed again, louder.

"Get lost, bitch!" he yelled. Everyone gathered around as he slammed the door in her face. "Sucker!"

She did not leave. She pounded on the door, screaming and crying at the same time.

"Stop it, you tramp!" he called from the other side of the door. "If you don't, I'll call the cops!"

* * * * *

"I want to keep this baby," Juliajo told her parents that Saturday. "I know I can make it work."

"Dear," her mother began, "I know how you feel, but you hardly make enough as it is. How can you support yourself and a baby?"

"Come home to us," her father chimed in. To her mother, he said, "We'll help all we can, Frances. Juliajo, our home is yours, too. You go ahead and have the baby, Juliajo, even though the father is a son-of-a-gun. Boy, I'd like to kill him for what he did to you. But what's done is done, right Frances? It's her baby, and our first grandchild."

The decision was made, plain and simple. Her parents understood and supported her pregnancy. She moved back in with them, and worked until April, when her labor pains began.

* * * * *

"Arlene!" Juliajo smiled warmly at her newborn daughter cradled in her arms. "I'm going to call you 'Arlene,' after my beloved grandmother, Adeline, may she rest in peace."

She looked down at her baby daughter. She looked so much like Juliajo, with blonde hair and dark eyes that opened up wide, sparkling at the world.

"I love you, Arlene, my precious darling. I always will."

She meant what she said. She kissed the baby's cheek and held her close to her breast. The love she felt would endure always.

CHAPTER TWO

Though she had the support of her parents, Juliajo worked hard at her job and taking care of Arlene. The hours were long, and she often came home tired, but Juliajo never neglected the baby. She fed her, changed her, and gave her baths. She just loved touching her soft, pink baby flesh. She dried her in a towel and cradled her. She bought her toys and played with her. She sang her lullabies and kissed her good night.

Arlene was a happy baby. She would try to grab her mother's earring and look up at her with eyes so much like her mother's that said, "I love you, Mama."

She slept most of the day and ate her meals regularly without difficulty.

Arlene was not yet one year old when she said her first word, 'Mama.' She started to walk at that time, as well. She would fall, but always managed to pick herself up and try again. How Juliajo loved watching her grow and listening to her.

Her vocabulary consisted of one hundred words by age two. She became toilet trained then, and asked for 'big girl pants,' her first full phrase as she took her diapers off the racks and threw them in the garbage pail.

Juliajo's parents loved their only granddaughter. She was so much like Juliajo, they remarked from time to time. She was always restless—never quiet, never still. She laughed and talked endlessly, climbing on all the furniture, giggling, knocking things down.

Life was not bad at all, Juliajo felt, despite everything.

When Arlene turned three, however, things changed. Juliajo's father had a stroke and died shortly thereafter.

The funeral was brief—just the family and some neighbors.

Juliajo did not know how she, her mother, and Arlene were going to manage. His pension was only enough to pay for the funeral. How would they live?

* * * * *

A week later, Juliajo took her usual lunch break at a nearby café, ordering a tuna sandwich and coffee.

She noticed a tall, wavy dark-haired, brown-eyed man walking into the café. He took a seat in the next booth. He did not seem to notice Juliajo, but when she got up, she dropped her purse and its contents fell out on the floor.

The man saw this and bent down to help her. Their eyes met. Juliajo giggled shyly. "Oh, that's okay, thanks anyway," she said.

"No," he persisted. "Let me help you."

He continued gathering her belongings and handed them to her with his hand extended. She took them, and then shook his hand.

"Charles Durning," he introduced himself.

"J-Juliajo. Juliajo Gilbert," she stammered excitedly.

"How about dinner tonight?" he asked.

Juliajo was flattered, but hesitant. She did not answer at once.

"Well?" he persisted.

She nodded.

"About eight at your place?"

"I live with my mother."

He was undaunted by that statement and asked for her address, which she gave him.

"Here's my card," he said. He reached into his pocket for it. It said, DURNING'S WOMEN'S WEAR, CHARLES FERDINAND DURNING, PRESIDENT,

Juliajo still felt leery. She felt she had to tell him about Arlene; it would not be right if she did not.

"There's something I must tell you."

Charles stopped her with his hand and said, "Over dinner, okay?"

She nodded reluctantly, then blurted it out. "I have a three-year-old daughter," she paused. "I'm not married. I never was," she finished.

He laughed. "So, what's that got to do with us? I'll be glad to meet her. I think you should go back to work now, before one of us changes our minds.

He left, and she stood there feeling attracted to this stranger, Charles Durning.

* * * * *

Over dinner that night, Juliajo told him she was a salesperson at the dollar store.

"A beautiful girl like you with a job like that? Oh, come on!" he said.

"It's true. I can't do anything else."

"Have you ever thought of modeling? You have the body for it. You'd be great."

She blushed coyly.

"You could work for me. You'd make as much as five hundred dollars a day. It would help you with your mother and daughter."

"Oh, I couldn't. I appreciate the offer, but I couldn't."

"You're doing it, Miss Gilbert. I said so. I remember this afternoon, seeing you. I told myself you'd make a perfect model. Tell your boss tomorrow you're leaving the thrift store."

Juliajo did not know what to say. They were attracted to each other. He didn't maul or force her. He was, it seemed, trying to make her life better.

She told him about Spencer.

"The bastard!" he said defiantly. "Forget him. Let's go to a movie. It's still early."

* * * * *

Frances was shocked when she heard the news.

"You hardly know him. How could you do this? He could be a con artist or a rapist or a madman."

"He isn't, Mother. He gave me his card."

Frances was doubtful, yet she wanted her daughter to be happy and they did need the money. Finally, Frances gave in,

"Take care of yourself and my granddaughter," she said.

The work day was long and hard. Juliajo had to be in by eight in the morning and never got home until nine at night, but she loved it. She modeled all the latest fashions—dresses, gowns, skirts, tops, pants, sweaters. Charles would watch her walk up and down the aisles in front of prospective clients, his heart heavy, his mouth watering as he watched her small but shapely figure in the low-cut tops and dresses. He could not keep his eyes off her. He wanted her.

And she him.

His eyes were large, piercing, and gleaming. His dark hair was thick and wavy. He had bushy eyebrows, an oval-shaped face, broad shoulders, and perfect features. 'Does he like me?' she wondered.

At night, he would go home and think of her—of her smile, her sparkling eyes, small mouth, perky nose, and her platinum-blonde hair on her head with opal pearl earrings dangling beneath.

* * * * *

Weeks passed, then months. Then it turned into two years. Juliajo was doing well as a model. Money was coming in, and business prospered. Charles told her the company hadn't done as well before Juliajo came. It was her, Juliajo, who brought in business and increased customers. That was good. Charles was happy. Juliajo was working out. Charles knew she would. He was pleased with the way things were turning out, but he still thought of his personal feelings for Juliajo.

Juliajo, too, was pleased. However, her concern was for her mother. She was getting old and caring for Arlene was becoming too much of a responsibility. Frances got arthritis in her legs and couldn't move as fast. She began to forget important things such as shutting off the gas.

Arlene was starting kindergarten, excited about learning. Juliajo told her about the games she would play and the children she would meet in her class. Juliajo had already taught her the letters of the alphabet, and Arlene learned to print her name. She also knew the names of all the colors.

Juliajo bought her daughter reading and writing books with pictures, teaching her. Numbers came harder, but Arlene kept at it. Juliajo also bought math workbooks, and never got tired of teaching her. Arlene was always eager to learn.

Juliajo bought CDs and taught Arlene about music. She read her a fairy tale every night.

Arlene was a happy child, adored by both her mother and grandmother.

Frances' health was failing, however. Juliajo tried telling herself that her troubles were only temporary, and that Frances would get better soon, but she wasn't.

One night as Juliajo came home from work and put her key in the lock of the door, she heard screaming and crying. It was Arlene. Juliajo rushed in and ran toward the child. She hugged her closely to her breast and asked, "Arlene, what's wrong?"

She didn't stop crying.

"Arlene!" she yelled. "What happened? Where's Grandma?"

Arlene stopped and turned her head. There was Frances.

"Mother!" Juliajo cried.

Frances was on the floor, holding a pot, her eyes open, not moving. Juliajo shook her wildly, calling, "Mother! Mother!"

Frances did not stir.

Frantically, Juliajo dashed toward the telephone and called Emergency, crying as she screamed for an ambulance. Arlene was screaming and sobbing, too. Noises were heard in the hall. It was the neighbors. One rang the bell. Juliajo opened the door. Everyone was asking questions all at once, but she couldn't answer them.

There was a man's voice about twenty minutes later, calling, "Police, let us through!" They pushed their way toward Juliajo.

"She's in there!" Juliajo pointed the way.

They went in, with Juliajo following. An EMT took out his stethoscope and placed it on Frances' heart. He looked up at Juliajo.

"She's dead, Miss Gilbert," he stated flatly. "Heart failure," he diagnosed.

Juliajo was in a state of shock. She did not cry or scream, but just stood like a statue.

Arlene came over and put her arms around her mother's neck, holding her. They held each other, saying nothing.

Later, Juliajo called Charles, asking for two weeks leave. He agreed and sent his condolences.

* * * * *

As with her father, the funeral was small and quiet. Charles was there. Juliajo bent over the casket and kissed her mother on the forehead.

"I love you," she whispered. Arlene was with her, watching.

"Where's Grandma going now?"

"With the angels in Heaven, darling."

"Why? Why won't she come home with us? I love her," Arlene said.

"God wants her with him."

Arlene asked more questions. Juliajo grew tired. "Honey, it's God's will that Grandma be with him. Remember, darling, Grandma loved us as much as we loved her. We'll remember the good times. No one can take those memories away. Do you understand?"

Arlene nodded, but Juliajo could tell she did not understand. Juliajo left the parlor holding Arlene's hand. She had to work the next day.

* * * * *

Juliajo found a day care center for Arlene. Juliajo asked if she could leave work earlier so she'd have more time to spend with Arlene. She felt she had to. She didn't want to neglect her daughter. She loved her, and Charles understood.

"You're a dear," Juliajo said to him, as she kissed him. He was tempted to kiss her back but avoided the thought.

'How I love her,' he thought.

About a month later, after everyone left, Juliajo was alone with Charles. She was straightening up the studio. Charles was watching her continuously. 'Wow!' he thought as he glanced at her from behind.

Finally, he just couldn't help himself. He grabbed her and kissed her on the cheek.

Juliajo was surprised. "Oh!" she exclaimed, dumbfounded. She turned toward him as he held her waist.

"I love you," he said.

Juliajo said nothing. She couldn't.

He kissed her on the lips.

She was still astonished.

"Your place or mine?" he asked.

She was still flabbergasted, but before she answered, he said, "Your place at eight sharp, okay?"

Juliajo smiled happily.

"It's settled! Eight o'clock tonight!"

Charles was in heaven. He would be with Juliajo tonight. His dream was coming true, and so was Juliajo's fantasy.

"I've been lonely for a long while," Charles said while drinking some wine while sitting next to Juliajo on her couch. "You are, too. I've never married, but I've got lots of love for the right woman."

Juliajo listened attentively. 'What's he trying to say?' she wondered.

"Juliajo, I've got an offer for you and your daughter. You both will be well provided for. Juliajo, I—" he could not continue.

"Go on," she said with interest.

"You're alone a lot. It's been a while since you've been with a man, but you deserve a good man—the right man. You won't have to pay the rent or bills, or anything."

Juliajo was astonished. She wanted Charles, and he wanted her, but what about morality and self-respect? She couldn't answer—not at that minute.

"Juliajo," he began, standing up, putting his glass down on the table. "I've loved you from the first time I saw you. You and Arlene are alone in this apartment. It's small and cramped. You'll move in with me. Arlene will have anything she wants and needs." Finally, he got down on his knee with a ring and nervously asked, "Juliajo, will you marry me?"

Juliajo wanted to. She loved him, and he loved her. Much had to be considered. Her furniture would be put in storage. She'd have to notify her property owner. She needed time to prepare.

She then said quietly, "I've always loved you. It's a dream come true. Oh, yes, Charles," she said gleefully, getting up and embracing him.

"Let's set the date!" she stated.

* * * * *

A month later they were married at the Justice of the Peace in a small courthouse.

* * * * *

As she was packing, Juliajo looked around the familiar surroundings she had grown up in. Now she was a woman of twenty-three years, with an adorable child and the man of her dreams.

Charles' apartment was on the East Side of New York, with carpets of red and black throughout the halls and bedrooms. There were antiques of all kinds, including a chiming grandfather clock in the foyer. The living room was done in black and white, and furnished with a love seat and a royal-red velvet couch and marble coffee table. The master bedroom had a heart-shaped bed with mirrors covering all the walls, and a dresser of white marble.

They decided to make Arlene's room pink, with a floral canopy bed with satin sheets. She'd have stuffed animals and different dolls throughout the room. Charles bought unfinished furniture and painted it hot pink, with large flowers on the sides.

For the first five years, Charles wined and dined his wife and took her to shows, plays, movies, and the opera. Each birthday, he bought her a piece of jewelry. He hired a house cleaner. Juliajo was not to lift a finger. They cuddled in bed and frolicked under the blankets like children.

Charles treated Arlene like his own daughter. He bought her toys, books, and games, as well as frilly dresses. He read to her, told her stories, took her to the zoo, and watched her feed the animals.

Arlene adored her stepfather. She never wondered about her own father. Juliajo told her he had died before she was born. She wouldn't understand the truth, Juliajo reasoned. When she reached puberty, she'd realize. Juliajo was content with Arlene and Charles' relationship, with Charles becoming the father Arlene never had.

Arlene spent much time at home. When Juliajo would go out shopping or on an errand, Arlene would remain alone with Charles. ALONE.

Juliajo's paradise was to be shattered.

CHAPTER THREE

"Mama! Mama!" eleven-year-old Arlene called from the bedroom. Juliajo was in the bedroom with Charles, cuddling in front of the television.

Arlene continued, "Mama! Mama!"

Charles released Juliajo gently as she moved off the bed after giving him a quick peck.

"I must see what Arlene wants. I'll be right back, darling."

"Sure, honey."

Juliajo went into the bathroom and saw Arlene holding her nightgown up. Her underpants had red stains on them. Arlene got frightened.

"Mama," she cried. "I'm bleeding to death. Please, help me!"

Juliajo laughed as she examined the panties. Arlene stared wide-eyed and frightened.

"Mama, please!" she cried.

Juliajo smiled at her daughter.

"Don't be upset, honey. You're a woman now. I became one at twelve."

"What do you mean?" Arlene was puzzled.

Juliajo began to explain. "You've started menstruation—your period. You can have babies now. Your body will be changing."

Arlene listened attentively to her mother. Juliajo took her to the bedroom by the hand.

"Stay here and wait. I'll be right back."

As she left, Charles was in the hall.

"What's going on?" he asked.

"Arlene's a woman now, Charles—a woman. Can you believe that? My baby!"

He said nothing as she passed him by.

Charles then went into Arlene's room.

"Well, Princess, you're a woman now," he said quietly.

Arlene stared at him and said nothing.

"You're a lady now," he reiterated.

She turned from him. He stayed a few more minutes, then left.

Juliajo came in with some books. She showed Arlene each one.

"Arlene, come here," she motioned as she sat on the bed. Arlene cuddled up to her as Juliajo showed her pictures of men's and women's body parts, and how a baby was made. She explained each aspect carefully. Arlene seemed to comprehend.

Juliajo felt a sudden need to tell Arlene about Spencer.

"Arlene, darling," she began carefully. "I lied to you, but I want you to know it was for your protection. Now that you're a lady, I think you should know the truth about your father."

Arlene listened, then asked. "What about him? You said he was dead."

Juliajo was silent for a while. She looked away from Arlene, then got up and paced the room. She looked out the window, then went back to Arlene on the bed.

"I was only seventeen and in love—or at least I thought I was. Spencer was tall, rugged, and charming. He lied to me. When I told him I was pregnant, he called me a bitch and tramp. He didn't care about you. I'm telling you this now because I feel you'd understand. Before, you could not."

Arlene continued listening as Juliajo went on, "Arlene, that's not important now. What's important is that I love you and so does Daddy Charles. He's the only father you'll ever have and though he's not your biological father, he loves you, and I love you more than anything in this world. I know you love me, too. Do you understand?"

Arlene threw her arms around her mother's neck and kissed her cheek. They held each other for a while.

"I love you, Mama," Arlene said sincerely.

"I'll get you some sanitary napkins and fresh panties. I'll show you what to do, okay?"

Arlene nodded as Juliajo left the room.

Charles came back and stared at Arlene.

"How's about a kiss for your dad, little lady?"

Arlene sat with a blank stare and did not answer.

"No one will ever love you like I do, Arlene, my darling princess," he said.

CHAPTER FOUR

Though she was only eleven, Arlene began noticing changes in her body, as her mother said she would.

She'd stand in front of her full-length mirror in her underwear and examine the firmness of her tiny breasts and feel her nipples standing erect. She felt the pubic hair between her legs, and at times would get the urge to touch herself there and everywhere.

Her hair was of a deep yellowish blonde—a thick mane flowing down her shoulders. Her deep, dark eyes shone large and wide as she watched herself growing into a woman.

Most of the girls in her class noticed these changes in Arlene and would talk of them—physical changes, sex, and boys. That did not interest Arlene. She was not outgoing. She didn't associate with the other girls. She was a quiet, shy child who just did her work and bothered nobody. No one mentioned her behavior to her or her mother. She stayed mostly to herself.

* * * * *

There was going to be a school dance in a week. Juliajo and Charles decided to buy her a dress for the occasion, with shoes and a small evening bag. Juliajo said she could wear lipstick, but nothing more. She was only eleven. Juliajo felt a need to set a limit. Arlene might be a woman physically, but emotionally she was just a little girl, inexperienced with life and the world around her.

Was she really?

Arlene knew, and so did Charles, but Juliajo remained in the dark.

* * * * *

It was Friday, the night of Arlene's first dance. There was much excitement.

Juliajo was fixing the collar of Arlene's pink eyelet dress with puffed sleeves and lace.

"Look at yourself," she said as she posed Arlene in front of her mirror, "Oh, you're so beautiful." She bent over and kissed her.

Charles was watching from the doorway. Juliajo turned toward him and said, "Isn't she, Charles? Doesn't she look beautiful?"

He nodded and smiled.

"Get your Smartphone camera. I must take a picture. She's so beautiful with her hair up in curls and in that dress."

Charles said, "Yes, honey, but I have a surprise for Arlene." From behind his back, he produced a pink corsage.

"Oh, Charles, how thoughtful." She took it and pinned it on her daughter's dress.

"There," she stated. "Now, I'd like a picture."

Charles got his camera and told Arlene to smile. She had to force herself to smile. Charles was ogling her.

"Come on, Princess, give a big smile for your dad."

Finally, she did.

"There," he announced as he clicked the camera. He turned to Juliajo and said, "Now, I'd like a picture of my two favorite ladies together."

"Oh, Charles, please," Juliajo said. She laughed nervously.

Charles was persistent. It was hard to resist him.

Finally, Charles wanted a picture of himself with Arlene. Arlene cringed at the thought. She did not want him near her.

"Smile!" Juliajo exclaimed.

Arlene's smile was strained. Charles had his arms around her waist as he said gleefully, "Cheese!"

"Let me drive her to the dance now. It's getting late," he said.

"Fine, darling," Juliajo stated, as she bent over to Arlene and kissed her. "Have an enjoyable time, honey. I want a full report, all right, sweetheart? Drive carefully, Charles."

* * * * *

They were off. Juliajo stood and stared. Arlene seemed disturbed, Juliajo thought. It was just growing pains, she reasoned. She was a normal child with the usual problems of adolescence. It was nothing.

Or was it? Juliajo didn't know for sure.

* * * * *

Arlene sat on a bench with a couple of other girls, watching the others dance. She really didn't care about dancing, and she did not want to go to this dance. Arlene knew no one would talk to her or ask her to dance. She had only gone to please her mother.

She saw some boys go over to the other girls, asking them to dance. She still sat alone.

"Hey, Arlene," a girl, Lee, nudged her and said. "Look!" She pointed. "That's Sheldon Sherman. I think he likes you."

Arlene turned and saw Sheldon, but she did not respond.

Lee went on, "He's watching you. I bet he wants to ask you to dance."

Still, Arlene said nothing, but Lee kept at it. "Why don't you go over to him? He's bashful."

At that point, Sheldon came over to Arlene and shyly asked, "D-d-do you w-want to dance?"

Lee nudged her. "Go on. He asked you to dance. Go ahead."

Reluctantly, Arlene got up. Sheldon took Arlene's hand as he led her to the dance floor.

He put his arm around her, with her hand on his shoulder. She shuddered, though, she tried to be sociable. She was uncomfortable in the present situation and wished she were home with her mother.

She watched the other girls dance. They hugged the boys, their arms around their necks, moving closer and closer as they danced.

She could not wait till the dance was over so she could go home and be safe and unharmed. It went on, one dance after another. Sheldon and she danced every dance together.

Finally, Sheldon asked her if she'd like some punch. Arlene shrugged and went with him. He poured her some, and they drank it.

"What's your favorite subject?" Sheldon asked, trying to initiate conversation.

"English," she replied blandly.

"I like lunch and physical education," he said with a laugh. He waited for her to respond, but she didn't, so he went on.

"How do you like the teachers? I think they're all yucky."

She said nothing, but she did smile slightly at Sheldon's remark. She listened to him. He had reddish-brown hair, hazel eyes, and dimples. He was cute, she thought. He wasn't so bad. He was just being friendly and was interested in her.

"Have you ever been to SeaWorld?" he asked.

"No," she replied.

"Well, you should go. They have these dolphins that can sing. Do you believe that? They even do math. Really!"

Arlene continued listening. It was fun hearing what he had to say.

"There are all diverse kinds of fish, too—all colors. All weird sizes. You should go, honestly."

"It does sound like fun," Arlene stated quietly.

They talked on, sitting and drinking punch. He got up and got her a sandwich, which she took and began eating slowly.

That was that—the end of Arlene's first dance.

* * * * *

When she got home, Juliajo was waiting eagerly to hear about her night. Arlene didn't acknowledge her mother.

"I'm tired, Mama," she said. "I want to go to bed."

A pained look crossed Juliajo's face.

"What's wrong, darling? What happened?"

Arlene walked away from her mother, went to her room, and closed the door.

"She's just tired, Juliajo—let her be. She's had a rough day," Charles said.

Juliajo was not to be dissuaded. She marched straight to Arlene's room, but then thought, 'she is tired, we'll talk in the morning. Charles is right.'

Charles came into Arlene's room about an hour later. She was in bed. He put his hand on her arm. She jerked away. He touched her face gently.

"You're so lovely, Princess—so very beautiful. Those boobs!" He touched her there, and she screamed.

"Get out of here! Don't you touch me, ever! I hate you!"

He quickly covered her mouth. Juliajo came in.

"What's wrong?" she asked.

Startled, Charles turned and said, "Nothing—nothing at all. I was just saying 'good night.'"

CHAPTER FIVE

Mrs. Greenworth, the school psychologist, had sent for Arlene to come down to her office. The secretary knocked on her door, and told her Arlene was here.

"Send her in," said Mrs. Greenworth.

Arlene shyly came in.

"Close the door and have a seat, dear."

Arlene did so. Mrs. Greenworth smiled at her and said, "Don't be frightened. I just want to talk with you."

"Have I done anything wrong?"

"No, dear. I'm just concerned about you. Your teachers say your work is very good, but that you don't associate with any of the other girls in the class. Mrs. Wall, from English is especially concerned."

"Why?"

She took out a composition from her desk that Arlene had written. It had received an A. It was well organized and developed, but its subject matter was upsetting.

"Mrs. Wall was perturbed at your composition. Tell me, Arlene, what's wrong?"

Arlene sat silently, while she bent her head. She wanted to talk but could not.

"Is everything all right at home?"

Again, silence.

"Something's wrong, isn't it? Don't be afraid to tell me. If you tell me, I can help you. That's my job."

"My dad—stepfather, he—"

"Go on, dear. He what?"

"He's been messing around with me," Arlene blurted out.

"I figured that from your paper since it dealt with sexual relations between older men and little girls. It's a tough problem, but it can be helped. I'll talk with your mother—"

"NO!" Arlene shouted. She was frightened. This was her stepfather—the only father she knew, the man who supported her and loved her mother.

"Arlene, you'll have to tell her, but if you want, I'll go with you. I can help. I know people who have experience helping children dealing with sexual abuse. Please, Arlene, it's the only way."

* * * * *

Arlene was afraid. Mrs. Greenworth was with her in the living room. Juliajo came into the house and was startled. Mrs. Greenworth got up and extended her hand. "Mrs. Durning, I'm Mrs. Greenworth, the school psychologist. I'm here because I'm concerned about Arlene."

"What's wrong? What's happened?" Juliajo asked.

"Arlene has told me some very disturbing news," she paused. "I think Arlene should tell you. I told her I could help if you knew."

"What's wrong?" Juliajo asked.

Arlene began slowly. "Daddy Charles has been having sexual relations with me."

A clouded expression crossed Juliajo's face, an expression Arlene had never seen before.

There was silence.

"Mrs. Durning, you must understand. I have to report this. It is the law."

Juliajo exploded with rage, "You better not," she grabbed the woman's hand before she had a chance to call Social Services on her cell phone. Mrs. Greenworth was frightened. She knew she had an obligation, but she was terrified of the girl's mother. She was between a rock and a hard place.

"Get out of my house!" Juliajo demanded, pointing at the door. "Get out! And don't you dare come back or you will be very sorry. My daughter is just a troubled teen-age girl and is making up lies to get attention and start trouble!"

"Mrs. Durning . . ." she began again.

"Out!" Juliajo ordered. "Or I'll call the cops."

"Please, I want to help."

Juliajo pushed her toward the door, opened it, and shoved her out. She then faced her daughter with boiling rage, "And you, go to your room!"

"Mama!" she cried. "It's true! I swear!"

Juliajo paid her no heed.

"Go to your room, now!"

Arlene started screaming. "Mama! Please!" She obeyed her mother, tears streaming down her face.

"And not another word out of you. Do you hear me?"

Arlene continued crying. Juliajo stood there, saying and doing nothing.

Charles walked in the door, hearing Arlene. "What's wrong?" he asked.

"Nothing," she stated firmly. "Nothing at all. It's just growing pains, that's all."

* * * * *

Later that night, Juliajo went into Arlene's room and sat down on the edge of her bed.

"Arlene," she began quietly, "how could you do this to me and to Charles? He has been the only man who will ever be a father to you. He loves us. We live in his house, and he provides for us. Now, I understand that you are perturbed. You're becoming a woman—a woman with normal desires and feelings. I've had them too, but don't take it out on Charles. It's not fair."

Arlene turned her back to her mother. She didn't answer or face her. She was silent and still.

Juliajo wanted to touch Arlene and tell her she loved her—to hold her, cradle her in her arms, and comfort her—but she couldn't. Things would never be the same for them again. This saddened Juliajo deeply. Quietly, with a pained look on her face, she got up and closed the door behind her.

CHAPTER SIX

For the next two years, Arlene was no longer shy and frightened with her mother. She hardly spoke to her. As for Charles' advances, she took them like a true soldier.

'Damn them!' she said to herself. 'All my own mother does is sleep with that bastard thinking he's my father. He's nothing but a shit head, and all she is is a bitch in heat.'

Juliajo never told Charles what happened. She loved him, worked for him, and did his bidding. Arlene changed. She became rebellious and vulgar. She was in control now, not to be defeated.

After school, she met Lee and some of the other girls.

"See this!" Lee held up a cigarette. "Try it, Arlene," she said.

Arlene was interested. "What is it?"

"Just try it. Smoke it like this." She demonstrated by putting it in her mouth. "Go on, Arlene, try it."

Arlene was hesitant, but took it and put it in her mouth, then inhaled, then exhaled. She sighed. She felt good.

Lee and the others watched. Arlene was getting high.

Arlene liked how they dressed in low-cut blouses with short skirts that just barely covered certain body parts. They also wore high-heeled leather boots, covered their faces with bright-colored eye shadow, and put a lot of powder on their faces. They applied lipstick, as well. Their nails were always dripping scarlet.

Arlene wanted to become one of them, and she did. She took the allowance Charles gave her and began buying those kinds of clothes, as well as make-up. She let her beautiful hair go, hardly washing it, letting it hang loose and uncombed.

Juliajo was aghast. She could not believe she was the mother of this girl. The new Arlene was proud and headstrong.

Juliajo was angry, too. Why was Arlene doing this? It was getting out of hand. It wasn't growing pains. She was just a rotten kid.

Every morning there was a fight.

"Get that crap off your face and change your clothes, now!"

"NO!"

Juliajo screamed, "Do it!"

"No!" she screamed again.

At that, Juliajo raised her hand to slap her, but didn't. Arlene stood with her arms folded, laughing. "You don't have the guts. Why don't you hit me? Go on, hit me? Hit me! I dare you!"

She gloated and left the apartment. Juliajo stood transfixed with tears in her eyes. "My baby," she said. "My darling, precious Arlene."

* * * * *

Arlene met Lee, Randi, and Sue every day after school, and they would smoke and talk about boys.

"I did it a lot of times with a lot of guys," Lee bragged. The others giggled. So did Arlene. They spent time together after school and all evening.

Juliajo was getting fed up. She wanted to beat her—kill her—make her stop. She was powerless. Still, she loved her, more than anything, even if this girl could not be her beloved daughter, her precious little darling.

Charles did nothing at all. Juliajo complained to him, and he shrugged. He began ignoring her, hardly speaking to her. Their lovemaking took place less often, with no feelings of love and tenderness present.

Arlene's grades also suffered. Juliajo received calls from the school; Arlene was cutting classes and skipping school. She talked to Arlene, tried to reason with her and to become her friend again, but Arlene rebuffed her mother.

"I don't know what to do anymore," Juliajo said to Arlene. "I love you, Arlene . . . you know that."

Arlene stared at her with angry eyes. "No, you don't! You never did! You hate me! Everyone knows it, too!"

"Arlene, please!" Juliajo said. "Please, darling, please don't say that. It's not true. It isn't. I swear to you. I love you. Please come back to me." She held her arms out. "Come to me."

Arlene left the room, entered her bedroom and blasted the speaker. Juliajo stood, crying bitterly, as though her heart would break. She had lost her daughter. She felt she'd die.

To make matters worse, Charles' treatment of Juliajo got worse. He paid no attention to her. He did not touch her, kiss her, hold her, or comfort her. He came home, ate, read the paper, took a shower, watched television, then went to bed.

Juliajo had lost them both—the two people she loved the most in the world.

* * * * *

When Arlene was thirteen, matters became worse. Juliajo was called at work. Arlene was arrested for shoplifting leather jackets and boots with Lee and the others. Her truanting had become worse as well. Arlene cursed the teachers and threw a chair at one of the aides in the lunchroom.

That did it. Juliajo couldn't control Arlene anymore. Something had to be done once and for all. Even the principal was at the end of his rope. He was going to expel her.

Juliajo told Charles she had to leave. He said ok, and she drove away in her car to the precinct. She saw Arlene, who said and did nothing. Juliajo couldn't even look at her daughter.

The police and Juliajo talked for an hour. They let Arlene off this time, but she was not to go into that store again, or the next time it was going to be Juvenile Detention Hall.

Juliajo took her home. They rode alone in silence, dry-eyed and with blank stares, not facing each other.

Charles was home, but he wasn't alone. Juliajo was aghast. With him was a red-haired, blue-eyed woman. He was smiling, drinking, and smoking. The woman snuggled up to him, and he put his arm around her.

Juliajo was astonished but said nothing. This was not Charles, her Charles . . . her beloved Charles.

He turned and said, "Gina, this is the mother and her bastard offspring."

Gina laughed absentmindedly, still snuggling up to him.

"What's going on?" Juliajo asked.

Charles said nothing. He turned to Gina and said, "Excuse me, honey," he grabbed Juliajo's arm roughly and led her to the bedroom.

He slapped her face hard, repeatedly.

"Get out, bitch! Go on, get out! As of now, you are unemployed and homeless. Just get out—both of you."

Juliajo cried, not knowing what to say or do.

Charles saw Arlene standing by the door transfixed. He darted toward her, threw her on the floor, unzipped his pants, ripped off her pants, and put it in her. She screamed. He slapped her repeatedly.

"Get up, bitch! Get out of here, bitches! Now!"

Juliajo was horrified. Arlene had been telling the truth. It was true. Still frustrated, she got her things, and she and Arlene left. Charles and Gina laughed.

* * * * *

Juliajo was hurting. So was Arlene. They rode off in the darkness and rain until they got to a motel. They were drenched and crying. Juliajo had to call someone. But who?

Arlene sat on the bed in her slip. Juliajo glanced at her with a blank stare.

"YOU DID IT!" she yelled at her daughter. "YOU RUINED MY WHOLE LIFE!"

"Mama, please!" Arlene cried out.

Juliajo paid her no heed. She slapped her viciously across the face, repeatedly, then beat her with her fists. She grabbed the lamp cord and struck her with it. Arlene screamed as Juliajo beat her with it in a frenzy. She put it down, and then put her hands around her neck, trying to strangle her. Arlene continued sobbing.

"You bitch!" Juliajo yelled.

Crying, Arlene managed to say, "I hate you! I hate you!" She screamed it repeatedly as Juliajo tried to kill her.

Those were the last words Arlene said — for a long while, anyway.

The other tenants heard the noise. The police and an ambulance were called. Arlene was lying on the bed, battered and bruised. Juliajo was in a chair, distraught and drenched.

The EMT put his stethoscope on Arlene's heart. She was alive, trying to regain consciousness. She saw her mother.

Juliajo said, "Arlene!"

"She can't speak, ma'am. She's lost the power of speech," he stated sorrowfully.

Then a man and a woman entered the room and introduced themselves. The woman stated her name, "I'm Dr. Spencer," and indicating to the man beside her, "this is my partner, Dr. Kasher. We were notified about this situation and we feel both you and your daughter need to be admitted to the hospital for professional care, in-depth assessments, and treatment plans. We are both medical licensed psychiatrists. And afterward, we strongly feel you and your daughter need to be in an institutionalized setting. There is a school in Linwood that we happen to know has a very high successful rate for treating and curing adolescents with emotional disturbances. As for you," she continued, "we'll be sending you to Beekman. You're in deep need of psychiatric help."

Mother and daughter parted. It would be a long time until they met again.

PART TWO
RUBIN

CHAPTER SEVEN

"Oh, Andrew, I love you," Lana Baines remarked as they cuddled on the bed.

"Lana, let's get married. We'll be so happy together."

Lana laughed. "When, silly?"

"I don't know. You set the date, ok?"

Lana laughed again.

Lana was sixteen and Andrew was eighteen. Both were graduating this year, as Lana had skipped two grades.

Lana had long brown hair and hazel eyes. Andrew had jet black hair and black eyes. Neither were too short or too tall. They had met at band practice. She played clarinet. He played the cello. Lana was editor of the school paper. He was the captain of the football team. Both were honor students.

They had dated for over a year. Their first date was at Stechmann's, a hangout for teenagers. Movies thrilled them, and they went every weekend. They were together a lot. Sometimes they double dated. At other times, Andrew went drinking with his friends. Lana went shopping in the mall with girlfriends and they talked about the boys in the neighborhood.

Everyone was jealous of Lana and Andrew since they were always with each other. He'd call her, and they'd talk for hours on the phone. Their parents would get annoyed, but they were just kids having an enjoyable time, and they weren't doing anything wrong. They were young and in love.

* * * * *

One afternoon, Lana stood in front of her bedroom mirror feeling her stomach. She was two weeks late.

"Oh, boy," she thought to herself. "A baby."

She saw Andrew the next day.

"Let's get married now."

Andrew laughed.

"I mean it!"

He laughed again, not looking at her. His friends were there, drinking.

"You said I should set the date."

"Ha!"

"I'm pregnant."

He laughed again.

"I mean it," she said. "Really, I am. We must get married."

"Marry you?" he laughed, throwing his head back.

"You promised!" Her voice was shaking.

"Piss off!" he said, laughing.

Tears filled her eyes, and she ran from the schoolyard.

* * * * *

Lana's mother cried bitterly. Her father called her a tramp.

"Leave this house. I won't have a slut in my house."

Lana's mother begged, "Fred, it's her home. She needs us."

"She should have thought of that before she got herself in trouble."

"Fred!" she exclaimed.

He ignored her. "I'll give you some money till you find a job, but that's the last you'll hear from me."

Her mother was sobbing. "Please! She's our daughter."

"I have no daughter!" he stated firmly. "You're as good as dead. Did you think he was going to marry you? An easy lay is all you ever were to him, nothing more. Help her pack, Winifred. Go on. The sooner, the better. I don't ever want to see you again."

Then the phone rang. Fred answered it.

"Lana, telephone!" he called.

Lana came out to answer it. He turned from her, then went back to his chair and read the newspaper.

"Lana," Andrew addressed her on the telephone. "It's me. I called to propose marriage."

Lana smiled and hung up. She was happy. They were getting married.

* * * * *

A Justice of the Peace married the couple. Neither one's parents attended. When asked to kiss Lana, Andrew gave her a brief, apathetic kiss, but Lana didn't care. She was married and was having Andrew's baby.

The 'happy' couple was but an hour wed when Andrew revealed his true intentions. They were in the hotel when Andrew snarled, "I had a scholarship to study at Princeton and a promising career in physics, but I had to marry you, you slut," he said. He got a bottle of wine, poured some in a glass, and gulped it down furiously.

"Andrew, please," she begged.

He ignored her and drank some more.

"It's all your fault, you stupid bitch." He continued, "And with a bastard child. I'm probably not even the father. Ha!"

Lana began screaming, begging him to stop.

"I'll give you money when you need it. I rented an apartment. We'll have separate bedrooms. We won't even eat together. You go your way, and I'll go mine. The care of your little brat will be your responsibility, not mine. I only married you because my mother told me it was the honorable thing to do. Don't think because you're my wife it means anything special, or that I have any obligations toward you, because I don't. Ok?"

Lana was weeping bitterly. He had said he loved her and that they'd marry and be happy. Instead, she had a whole life in front of her of misery and helplessness in a loveless marriage.

* * * * *

Rubin Aaron Clemmens was born eight months after the marriage. He had jet black eyes and thick black hair. He weighed eight pounds and measured twenty inches from head to toe.

Lana held her precious bundle of joy, her baby, and looked at him with a gleam in her eyes. She smiled at him, rocking him back and forth in her arms.

As for Andrew, he was out with the boys at the bars, drinking and picking up girls. He was with a different girl every night. He didn't know of Rubin, nor was he interested in his son. When her labor pains began, a neighbor heard her screams and drove her to the hospital. They felt nothing but pity. What kind of man was Andrew? His wife was in pain, expecting his baby. Where was he?

The same neighbor drove her home. She offered him five dollars, which he refused. "Thanks a lot," she said.

"Anytime," he replied.

When she got out of the car, she saw Andrew standing by the door of their apartment. He snarled at her.

"Who was that man you were in the car with?" he demanded.

"Just Mr. Peterson, a neighbor. He drove me to hospital and back, that's all."

He slapped her face hard.

"Liar!" he said as he grabbed her arm and led her into the apartment.

When they got in, he threw her on the couch, causing her to almost drop Rubin.

"You'll hurt Rubin," she whimpered.

He ignored her, pushed the baby aside roughly, and slapped her repeatedly. Rubin started to cry.

"The baby!" she exclaimed.

"Get up, bitch!" he ordered. He was drunk and paid no attention to Rubin. He never would.

As time went on, though business was good at his father's drugstore, Andrew's money was running out. He squandered it on alcohol and slutty women. He'd spend the nights with whores, wining, dining, and drinking. When he was home, he'd beat Lana, sometimes in front of his friends and broads, and they'd all laugh.

That wasn't all. When Rubin was two, Andrew began abusing him with a belt or extension cord when he wet the bed, cried, or threw up his food. The more he cried, the more Andrew beat him. Their neighbors heard their screams—Rubin's and Lana's—but no one did anything.

Lana had no one to turn to. Her father had refused to help her. Her mother wanted to but was under the complete domination of her husband. Andrew's parents never acknowledged Lana or the baby. There was no one. She was alone and afraid.

* * * * *

A year later, the situation worsened. Drunk as usual and with business failing, Andrew hit Lana. Rubin began crying, so Andrew hit him, too—repeatedly. He reached for a bottle of whiskey and poured some in a glass. Then, as he drank it, he clutched his stomach, and fell down to the floor, struggling for breath.

Lana watched, horrified. "Andrew!" she yelled, trying to wake him. She called his name repeatedly. Frantic, Lana called an ambulance, and he was taken to the hospital.

Lana and Rubin went with Andrew. They stayed in the waiting room. She couldn't sit still. She got up and down. Up. Down. Up. Down. Rubin started crying. He didn't understand.

"Mommy!" he cried.

She felt helpless and held him to her. "My darling."

A doctor came in sorrowfully. "Mrs. Clemmens . . . he's dead."

Lana just stared. She didn't cry—she couldn't. She didn't know how to feel—upset or relieved.

Lana and her in-laws were the only ones at the funeral. Lana bent over the casket and saw Andrew's lifeless body. She still loved him despite everything. She kissed him like they did when they were still in school and in love, or what she thought was love.

"You filthy tramp!" her mother-in-law said sharply. "You killed him. You ruined his life!"

Lana said nothing. She took Rubin by the hand and left the parlor. She never saw her in-laws again.

CHAPTER EIGHT

Lana and Rubin left Hester Park with the money from the business. They were going to Brooklyn. Lana had sent in a resume for a seamstress position at a small dress firm and was to start immediately. She was grateful, for she needed money to support herself and Rubin.

The work wasn't hard. Her supervisor, Mrs. Adams, was kind and pleased with her work. She was offered the position of Head Seamstress over the other workers. This pleased Lana—it would mean more money.

When Lana worked, Rubin was left in the care of a babysitter. She had no problems with him. He was quiet and obedient and never showed any signs of disturbed behavior. He never really knew his father. His mother was kind to him, thus he used to draw her pictures with hearts and wrote, 'I love you' on them. She had taught him the alphabet, and he also learned to print his name.

When he was four, he asked her for a chemistry set. Lana was astonished. Why would a four-year-old ask for that? Most boys wanted trucks, boats, cars, or building blocks. No, he wanted a chemistry set. Lana got him one. He also asked for math and science books.

When he was five, and ready to start kindergarten, he was already doing second and third grade work. He would rather work in a lab than play with blocks or draw pictures like the other children. This made him different—a loner, shunned and friendless, but he was not perturbed. He knew what he wanted. He wanted to be a physicist.

His teacher told Lana to put Rubin in a special school for the gifted, for he was so smart. He was always reading, trying to solve puzzles, and figuring out problems. Lana was baffled by his extreme intelligence. Still, she felt he needed friends. His lack of them bothered her. She wanted him to be in kindergarten for the year, then she would decide.

Thus, he stayed in his school, alone and friendless, but content in his own little world.

He and his mother.

CHAPTER NINE

After her ordeal with Andrew, Lana refused to have any relationships with men. They asked her out, but she refused gently, saying she was busy and had other things to do. It was true. She had Rubin. He was the only man in her life, now and forever. She doted on him.

She bought him suits of blues and browns with matching shirts and ties. His shoes were always polished, his hair combed and neat. He looked like a miniature doll—a magazine model.

A decision about his schooling was made. Though he needed friends his own age, she decided to put him in a special class for the gifted in a regular school. This way he would receive the education he needed, plus he would be with others his age.

"My man," she called him, "My little man." She hugged and kissed him, and they lay together in bed watching television.

"Nobody will ever love you like I do," she told him.

"Come and give me a great big kiss." He did so.

He did well, as usual, in his studies, but still didn't attempt to make any friends. He was still alone . . . he and his mother.

* * * * *

When he was eight, he had a male teacher he admired. He was about six feet tall, with broad shoulders that showed his muscles. His eyes were of an almond-shape, medium-brown, and he had a thick head of brownish hair. He was David Owens, the science teacher, who smiled at Rubin in class. The other boys noticed and taunted him.

"He likes you. He loves you," they jeered over and over in the boys' room, hallway, and schoolyard during recess.

That was all he needed, a male teacher liking him. It wasn't right, he sensed, but he didn't know for certain. He never had any friends, and never would.

Often Rubin would hear the other boys talk of sex, love, and touching. Rubin never took part in the conversations they had. He knew nothing of the facts of life and was teased.

"Rubie," they told him, "Old man Owens likes you." They used words he knew nothing about. He was alone, still without a friend or a social life, and confused.

* * * * *

One day, Mr. Owens asked him to stay after class. Rubin didn't know why. The others snickered, but he stayed as told.

"I spoke to your mother. She says it's all right. I told her you'd be helping me after class," Mr. Owens told him.

'Help him? With what? How?' he wondered.

They went in his car to a lavish apartment in Flatbush.

"Don't be frightened," he told Rubin. "I'm your friend—the only one you'll probably ever have."

He finally had a friend, Rubin thought.

As they went in, Rubin noticed some magazines of nude men. He was puzzled. He saw statues of nude males—their genitals showing plain as day—and photos of young boys.

"I like to sculpt in my spare time," Mr. Owens announced. He showed Rubin a partially completed work of a teenage boy—tall with sharp eyes and firm bulging muscles.

Rubin noticed there were no pictures of girls or women. That was strange, he concluded, for men are supposed to like girls and vice versa.

"I don't see any pictures of young women, Mr. Owens. From what the others say, men are supposed to like girls. That's what they say."

David Owens said nothing for a while. He was ogling Rubin from head to toe, smiling.

"Don't believe everything you hear, Rubin. There are no laws saying whom a person must love."

"Oh," Rubin remarked stupidly. "Don't you like women, Mr. Owens?"

"Call me David. After all, we're going to be friends, right?" He slapped Rubin on the back playfully.

Rubin reiterated his question.

David did not answer.

"You're quite a young man," David remarked. "I think you're smart enough to know some things."

"What things?" Rubin was puzzled.

"You know . . . things," David said vaguely. He reached into his pocket and gave Rubin five dollars.

Rubin refused the money but was interested.

David put Rubin's hand on top of his zipper so he could feel the bulge of his penis. Rubin felt strange. It didn't seem right—his touching another man's organ. However, he did as he was told.

"Nice, isn't it?" David stated excitedly. "The five dollars is for that."

"It's getting late now," David mentioned later. "I'll be teaching you new things every day. You'll enjoy it, really you will, and I'll give you money for anything you want."

Rubin felt funny but was awed by David. Rubin had a friend. This arrangement was just between Rubin and David. Rubin told no one, not even his beloved mother, whom he adored—her breasts, soft and sweet, like David's penis. Oh, he felt good. Nothing perturbed him . . . for a while anyway.

Every day, for two years, Rubin went to David's place. Though he loved his mother, he felt close to David. Why shouldn't he? David was his friend. Rubin knew all this wasn't appropriate behavior, but he did not care. He was loved and had a friend.

"I was married once, but it didn't work out," David stated one day.

"What do you mean?" Rubin inquired.

David smiled and didn't answer at first, then he replied vaguely, "Sometimes things don't work out. That's life, you know."

He didn't go on, and Rubin did not pursue the matter. It made no difference in their relationship. He was content and happy.

* * * * *

However, one day their private little world ended. David was fired from his job. A neighbor in David's building saw Rubin and David together. She knew about David's same-sex attraction, and that he had murdered his wife and was an escaped convict. The whole building knew. Also, he was a procurer of young boys like Rubin. He lured them into sinful sexual activities.

Not only was Rubin alone and friendless once again—and taunted by the other children—his mother's behavior toward him changed as well. She no longer doted on him. Her hatred of men became apparent in her changed treatment of her son, whom she had adored.

"You like to play sex games, you little pervert? Okay, well, you'll play them with me!" she sneered.

She opened her blouse, exposing her breasts to him. "You like breasts, do you? You do. You better." It went on and on.

Another time, she lifted her dress, showing herself.

"Lick it, you little bum. I'm your old lady, and sometimes I get horny like your lover, Mr. David."

This scared Rubin. The two people he loved most in the world had both enticed him into sickly sexual games—games he knew were wrong and socially unacceptable.

David left him. His mother hated him and all men.

This went on through puberty. He had no friends, no interest in women. Other boys would show him pictures of naked women.

"Look at this one," one boy said, sneering as he showed him a picture of a girl with long red hair. Rubin paid no mind.

The boy continued showing other photos while jeering at him. Rubin showed no interest. He did not care one way or the other. Sex repelled him—with both men and women. He simply wasn't interested. Nothing excited him. He never noticed Dolly Lee, a girl in his class, who had a crush on him that everyone knew about.

Dolly Lee stared at him in class and in the lunchroom—Dolly Lee with honey-colored hair and blue-gray eyes.

One day, Rubin saw writing on his locker in big letters. 'Rubin the faggot and Dolly Lee forever.'

"Hey, fag," a boy called. "Why don't you suck Dolly Lee's tits? It'll do you good!"

Everyone in the cafeteria screamed and roared with laughter.

Rubin never told his mother, who continued her incestuous relationship with him.

* * * * *

When Rubin was twelve-and-a-half, he noticed white stuff coming out of his penis while masturbating, thus his organ became erect. He didn't know what it was. No one told him. He was in the bathroom near the commode trying to figure it out.

The bathroom door opened. Lana stood with her hands on her hips. "Ah-ha! So, you've taken to playing with yourself, have you, you little pervert!"

He turned and stared, aghast. His mother would punish him now for sure.

She smiled sarcastically, walking toward him slowly with an angry gleam in her eyes. He was standing partially naked, trying to cover up, but Lana pushed his hand away, letting his pants drop.

"You can make a baby now, darling Rubie," she mocked. She put her arms around him. "Don't worry, honey, I'll teach you everything you need to know—more than David, anyway. Now, how's about a kiss for your old lady?"

He turned away from her. She slapped him.

"Don't you turn your head away, young man. Now, how's about a kiss from my little man?"

He pecked her briefly.

"You call that a kiss? Come on, give me a real kiss! A good kiss!"

"NO!" he yelled.

She picked up a hairbrush and hit him hard. Rubin winced in pain.

"Do it!" she yelled again.

He didn't move.

"Do it, or I'll kill you!" she said, holding the hairbrush up in warning.

She had backed him against a wall. He closed his eyes, tightly gritted his teeth, put his arms around her, and kissed her right on the lips. She laughed hideously.

"Some lover boy you are, pervert! You'll sure make some girl happy one day, I can tell you that!"

Tears ran down Rubin's face as Lana laughed hysterically, her arms folded across her chest.

It went on and on. Rubin didn't know what to do. He couldn't avoid it. Every day there was a feel, a kiss, a touch, a peck. Lana watched him masturbate. She watched the seminal fluid coming out.

"That's what makes babies when you put it inside a girl, as if you didn't know!" she mocked him.

When a man would ask Lana out, she refused, saying she was busy. She was busy, all right—with her son, her little man. He was the only man in her life and always would be, forever. She was going to straighten him out and make him macho, and hers alone—no one else's.

"I'm the only woman in your life, now and always," she said gently as she stroked his organ in the shower.

They showered and bathed together. She touched him, felt him, made him love her passionately. He hated her now. Hated her. And he once loved her. Only her.

He now knew he was different from other boys, and always would be. He hated sex more and more each day. He'd never be normal like everyone else. He knew this. He wanted to be like other people, to enjoy life, have friends, go places, and be able to participate in talks with other boys his age, but it was impossible, and all because of his mother, who had once loved him the way a mother should love a son. She now treated him like her young lover, making him play games that he knew were sick and which disgusted him.

One day he was going to get even, once and for all. This couldn't go on. His mother was going to pay. He swore to it.

CHAPTER TEN

Dolly Lee, the girl in his class, still loved him. Though she knew of the incidents with David Owens, that didn't stop her. She found Rubin interesting. He was smart, and she thought about him endlessly. He knew all about computers and video equipment and animals—everything, except how to deal with people effectively.

Dolly Lee ogled him from the far end of the cafeteria where she wrote him love notes. He threw them away without reading them. On Valentine's Day, she sent him a large card with a red heart. She signed it, 'Love, your secret friend and admirer, D.'

He looked at it and heard snickers from the other boys. With rage in his eyes, he furiously ripped the card into pieces and threw it in the garbage. Dolly Lee smiled at him often as she passed him in the halls.

Rubin was thirteen now. He began shaving and noticing other signs of his developing masculinity. What was it Dolly Lee found attractive about him?

He felt guilty treating Dolly Lee this way, but he didn't know how to manage the situation. He had no one to discuss it with . . . not his mother—especially not Lana. She berated him. He had no friends, no male authority figures to look up to.

Come to think of it, he sort of liked Dolly Lee. She was endlessly trying to get him to notice her. He rebuffed her, but it didn't perturb her. She found him a challenge. Challenges were fun, she thought.

It was futile to even think of having a relationship with Dolly Lee or any girl. He couldn't see it. He wouldn't know what to do. He had never kissed anyone but his mother and David.

One day while Rubin was doing his homework, he heard the phone ring. It was probably a friend of his mother's, he reasoned. Who else?

He heard his mother answer the phone. "Who?" Lana asked into the telephone, annoyed.

Who was it? he wondered.

"All right, I'll get him," his mother said flatly.

Lana walked into Rubin's bedroom with her head up arrogantly. "Telephone! Some girl—Dolly Lee," she said, disgusted. "What's going on?"

He was puzzled. Why would she call him?

He got up and took the phone in the hall. Lana was there, listening to every word. She watched him.

He stuttered on the phone. He had never spoken to a girl before.

"I-I c-can't," he struggled to say, unable to go on. "I m-must go now." He hung up without saying good-bye.

Lana didn't take her eyes off him. His head was down. He couldn't face his mother.

"What was all that about?" she demanded.

"Nothing," he mumbled.

She grabbed his shoulders. "Look at me, young man! Who was that?"

Still with his head down, he replied, "Just some girl from school."

"Ha!" she laughed. "A girl. W-whew wee! You got a lover, don't you, you little bastard, you? Well, I'm better than she'll ever be. Did you sleep with her? Kiss her? Touch her?"

Rubin just stood there with his head down, not saying anything.

"Impregnate her?" she arrogantly asked. "You probably don't even know what to do with a girl, but I'll continue to teach you. You're my lover, you know. That Dolly Lee broad doesn't stand a chance. I'm better than she is! Much better! And now you'll leave me!" She was screaming.

She held her head. "I'll never have anyone again, ever!"

She left the room in tears. She was devastated. No other man would ever want her . . . just Rubin. She'd see to it that Rubin was hers and no one else's. Not Dolly Lee's, especially not Dolly Lee's.

Rubin couldn't and didn't understand what his mother was saying about no man ever wanting her. What about his father? He hardly remembered him. She had told him he had died from drinking too much, and that was it. She never explained that they had to get married, and that he didn't love her or Rubin. He didn't care about them. He had lied and pretended to be in love with her, drank, ran around with other women, and beat both of them.

She had told him none of this. She loved Andrew, no matter what. He used her, as her father had said, as a piece of ass. Rubin never knew any of this. He never asked. He didn't or seem to care.

Still, Dolly Lee liked him and wrote him love letters. Every time he began to read one, he'd hear an unkind remark. He'd blush and crumple the letters sorrowfully as he noticed the boys' mocking stares.

"Rubin the faggot loves Dolly Lee," they cheered throughout the school. "Dolly Lee loves Rubin boy, the queer."

* * * * *

Mr. Colby, the school psychologist, sent for Rubin after classes ended.

"Have a seat, Rubin," he told him. "I'd like to have a talk with you."

Rubin was frightened. "What did I do, sir?"

Mr. Colby laughed. "Nothing. I'm just concerned about you. Not about your work, which is excellent. You're a fine young man. You'd make a good president. What I'm concerned about is your social life. You don't associate with the other boys. Your teachers say they antagonize you—call you a queer and faggot. Is that true?"

Rubin nodded.

"Do you know why?"

Rubin looked down at his hands and shyly answered. "Because of Mr. Owens."

"I know about that, and it's things like that that can make children do and say cruel things. Do you understand?" He nodded again.

"Now, I want you to know something. If anyone bothers or harasses you, you tell me. That's what I'm here for, to help students cope. How's your life at home?"

Rubin shuddered at the question. He couldn't tell him the truth. Lana would kill him, call him a liar and a pervert.

"Fine," he finally replied.

"Are you sure? I mean, your mother doesn't have any support, being a single parent and all. It must be hard on her . . . and on you, without a father, especially at your age. Sometimes you may feel a need to talk things out. That's why I'm here, to be your friend. Anytime you need to discuss anything at all, just come to me. Ok?"

"Yes, sir," he responded dully.

Mr. Colby got up and extended his hand to Rubin, who briefly shook it. "Good luck—and remember, I'm here whenever you need me," he reiterated.

He had a friend now. Still, Rubin didn't feel comfortable. He wanted to tell Mr. Colby about his mother, but he couldn't. He had the opportunity—it was as plain as day.

* * * * *

One day, weeks later, Dolly Lee walked up to him in the hall.

"Hi!" she said brightly.

Startled, he turned. "Hi," he said dully.

She was smiling. He watched her, saying nothing. He was taking some books out of his locker. Dolly Lee watched him and tried to initiate a conversation.

"What's your next class?"

"Algebra. Room 208," he replied blandly.

"I have Spanish near there. Why don't we walk together?"

He slowly nodded and began walking with her.

"You don't talk much, do you? That's okay. I find the quiet type quite a challenge. How do you like school?"

"It's okay," he replied briefly.

"I think it's awful, but we must go. I simply can't wait till I get out of this place. Four long years, but I'll make it. I know you will, you're so smart. What's your favorite subject?"

"Chemistry," he answered nonchalantly.

"Chemistry! Yuk! I hate it. I like English, writing in particular. Do you like to write?"

"Not really."

"I didn't think so, with a mind like yours. I wish I were as smart as you. Your parents must be awfully proud. My parents, well, they're always on my case. You know what I mean."

At that point, Rubin said, "I have to go now."

Dolly Lee smiled sweetly and said, "Fine. It was really good talking with you. See you tomorrow, ok?"

"Yeah," he answered, in a low, barely audible voice. "Bye."

As they separated, Rubin heard a boy call out. "Looks like she really likes you, Rubin, baby. Hey, lover boy, fag!" He jeered across the hall.

Rubin didn't pay attention. He just walked into his classroom, saying nothing.

"She's really nice," he admitted to himself sincerely. "She's really nice and pretty."

He kept this to himself and told no one. He smiled to himself.

He wanted to see Dolly Lee again. His heart was beating fast. When would he see her again? he wondered.

He left school that day a happy young man in love.

CHAPTER ELEVEN

From then on, Rubin saw Dolly Lee in the hallway and in the cafeteria. They sat next to each other at lunch and walked to as many classes together as they could.

Rubin was still quite shy with her, but Dolly Lee did not give up on him. She didn't feel he was a lost cause. He had a cute smile that showed his perfectly straight white teeth. His dark eyes accented his smile when he saw her.

Dolly Lee was about average height, with the shape of an hourglass. She wasn't fat. She wasn't skinny. She was just right. Her eyes, a mixture of blue and gray, interested him. He often stared at them as though they were opals.

* * * * *

"Mother," Rubin said hesitantly one Thursday afternoon after coming home from school, "I'm going out tomorrow night to Stechmann's."

"Oh," she said, with an angry glare.

"I'm going to be with a girl, Mother, and nothing will stop me—not even you," he said bravely.

"What?" she yelled. "What girl?"

"Dolly Lee. Dolly Lee, Mother. She's a very nice girl, and sweet."

"Oh, really!" she remarked sarcastically. "Are you going to sleep with her? Get her pregnant? A pervert like you who likes male teachers."

He was undaunted by her. He was not to be defeated this time—not by his mother, especially.

"Mother, I'm going out," he reiterated as he got up from the kitchen table. "And that's that!"

Lana got up with fury and slapped him. He pushed her against the wall.

"You've hit me for the last time, Mother. Do what you want. Say anything you like. I'm going out. I'm going to go out wherever I want and with anyone I desire. I'm home too much. I want to enjoy life and be with others. Can't I make you understand that? What in the hell is wrong with you?"

Lana began weeping loudly. She was not used to her son talking to her like this—so bravely, so assertively. She didn't want to lose him, and she was afraid she was going to, forever. Then she'd be alone and friendless.

Would he turn out to be like his father? She prayed he wouldn't love 'em and leave 'em like Andrew had.

Sometimes she wished Andrew had completely left her. Instead, he had grudgingly married her and made their lives a living hell with beatings, drinking, and women.

Lana was the world's biggest loser in life. First she lost Andrew, now she was losing Rubin. Her little man, her son, the only man in her life.

This girl Rubin was interested in would take him away from her in any way she knew how. She didn't love him, Lana concluded hopefully. She would lead him on, tease him, and cajole him into sleeping with her. He would pretend to love her and want to marry her. She would have his baby.

She thought of what Rubin said to her, what he had decided to do. Go out with a girl—leave her for another girl.

"GODDAMN BASTARD!" she yelled, wanting Rubin to give in and be with her, and not with Dolly Lee or any other girl for that matter.

"GODDAMN BASTARD!" she yelled helplessly again. "DAMN YOU TO HELL! You'll be sorry! You just wait and see. Just leave me alone. Just go ahead and do it. See if I care!" Tears streamed down her face.

Rubin didn't answer her. He wasn't going to give in this time or any other time in the future. He was a man now. Lana would get over it, he thought. He knew it.

Or did he?

* * * * *

It was Friday night.

Rubin wore his tweed suit with a white shirt and grayish tie. He smiled as he looked in the mirror in his room.

Lana wept loudly.

"How can you do this to me? I love you more than anyone else ever will. No one loves you like I do, my little man."

'Little man.' He was close to fifteen years old, six feet tall, with broad shoulders and a muscular build that showed off his physique. He stood proudly and smiled. He was like everyone else. He was not a pervert, despite David Owens, a sickie.

His mother thought of him as queer—a sick person. She was the one who was sick. It was true, he thought. His mother was definitely sick, and he wasn't going to be used by her any longer. He loved her, but he needed a social life—boys his age and girls!

Lana was hurting. She accused him of wanting her to have a heart attack and die. He wanted her dead, she said. He didn't care about her. She cried and cried. Rubin left without saying 'good-bye.'

She stood in the hall crying and yelling to no avail. She was alone.

* * * * *

It was eleven p.m. Rubin came home smiling and singing. Obviously, he had an enjoyable time. As he opened the door, he saw his mother looking at him cross-eyed, an angry gleam in her eyes as she stood with her head up high and her arms folded firmly across her chest. She looked like a duchess—stern and arrogant.

He just stood there. Her eyes didn't leave his face.

"You bastard!" she spat out. "I'm the only woman in your life and always will be. Do you hear me?"

"Good night, Mother," he flatly said as he turned to leave the kitchen.

She grabbed him by the arms and dragged him to her bedroom. She threw him on the bed, threw off her bathrobe, and was completely naked in front of him. Rubin tried avoiding her gaze, but she pinned him to the bed.

"I bet your girlfriend doesn't have a body like mine. Mine is nicer, don't you think? Nicer than that broad's. Now, come on, pull down your pants. Go on, do it, you little sickie, you."

He refused.

"DO IT!" she screamed. "I want you to get it up!"

Rubin began crying, but to no avail.

"Come on!"

Rubin continued crying. He had to give in.

After a few minutes, Lana smiled. "There, my little lover, sonny boy. You're not so bad after all!" she gloated. "There's still hope for you yet," she laughed.

He had let Lana have her way with him again.

The weekend was hell for Rubin. Lana was after him constantly all weekend long. He didn't know what to do, but he knew something had to be done. He felt alone again.

* * * * *

Monday morning came. He saw Dolly Lee at school. He didn't return her greeting as he went to his algebra class. She caught up with him before he entered the room.

"What's wrong, Rubin?" she asked, concerned.

He didn't answer her. He just stared right through her.

"Are you mad at me?" she asked.

"I have a class now," he said abruptly, not answering her question.

"Rubin, what's wrong?" she asked desperately.

"Nothing. I must go." He turned and went into his classroom, leaving Dolly Lee standing in the hall perturbed.

He couldn't help it. He wasn't angry with her, but he was confused and frustrated, thanks to Lana. He was never going to be like everybody else. He knew it.

He liked Dolly Lee very much. He honestly and truly did. He wanted to be with her, but his mother forbade it. She forbade him to live, to be normal, to be like other people, to have a social life.

He knew his mother was a disturbed and troubled woman. It must be because of his father. He hardly remembered him. What kind of man was he? he wondered.

He would never marry, he decided. How could he, with his life the way it was? He hated women. Part of him did, anyway. Is that why David Owens was the way he was? Why did he kill his wife? Was his mother like Lana?

Rubin didn't know. He only knew he couldn't see Dolly Lee again, and it upset him that he couldn't talk to her. It hurt him deeply. Things deteriorated.

Dolly Lee came over to him in the lunchroom. Furiously, he jumped out of his seat and slapped her. She screamed, and there was a riot. He kicked her between her legs, pushing her against the wall.

Everyone laughed and screamed. Chairs, books, and food were thrown around. They cheered. "Stick it up! Stick it up!"

Dolly Lee was crying. Finally, Rubin couldn't help himself any longer. He ripped off her clothes, unzipped his pants, and put it in her.

She screamed in horror. He had sexually assaulted her right in front of everyone. He hated her.

"Bitch!" he yelled.

Dolly Lee was on the floor sobbing, undressed in front of everyone.

He just stared at her.

All the students and staff stood transfixed. Someone should have tried to stop it, but they were frightened. They knew not what to do.

Mr. Colby was called down. "What happened?" he asked.

"Rubin sexually assaulted Dolly Lee," a boy sang out.

He looked at Rubin. "Is this true?"

Rubin was ashamed, but remorsefully nodded. He didn't know why he had done it. He hadn't wanted to. He liked Dolly Lee. He didn't mean it.

An ambulance and the police were called. They put Dolly Lee in the car. Rubin was sent to the Police Precinct. He refused to talk. He simply couldn't.

Mr. Colby was sympathetic and wanted to help. "Why, Rubin? What made you do such a thing?"

"SHE MADE ME DO IT!!" he exclaimed finally. "SHE MADE ME DO IT!!"

"Who?" Mr. Colby asked.

Finally, it came out after all these years about his mother and their relationship, sick as it was. He described his mother's sexual abusiveness toward him in detail.

Mr. Colby was stunned. Lana seemed like a nice person. They had met on Open School Night. However, he believed Rubin, for Rubin had never lied in the past.

Lana had to come down to the precinct to pick Rubin up. Mr. Colby looked at her in disgust.

"Your son told me about how you treat him, Mrs. Clemmens."

Lana's face contorted into rage. "He's a liar. That's all he is, a goddamned liar!"

"Mrs. Clemmens, you can be helped, honestly. You can go to therapy."

She was angry. She was such a nice lady. Who would suspect her, of all people, of such things? She had a gleam in her eyes and stared at Rubin. No one would believe him, she thought. No one.

Then the police chimed in. "We decided to have your son go to court one month from this Wednesday. They will make a final decision as to whether to put him in Juvenile Hall. In the meantime, he'll be suspended from school. I strongly suggest you get him a tutor. Also, Mr. Colby recommended a psychiatrist with a good reputation for both of you. I strongly advise you, Mrs. Clemmens, to go. It'll help you deal with your problems."

Lana continued her fury. "How dare you tell me what to do! He's my son, and I'll do what I damned well please!" She grabbed Rubin's arm and led him to the door roughly.

"Go on!" she demanded. "Get in the car!"

Mr. Colby and the police officer stared helplessly.

* * * * *

When they got home, Lana began undressing herself.

"Come on, pervert. Why don't you do it? Come on! Rape me! Rape me!" she screamed at him.

She grabbed him and forced him to get on top of her.

Finally, it happened.

"See this, Mother?" He showed her a knife from his pocket. "See it?"

Lana became frightened. He came closer and closer to her until she was backed against a wall, her eyes glazed in horror.

"RUBIN!" she yelled. "You're crazy!"

"No, Mother. It's you who's crazy, not me. You made me this way, and you're going to pay for all the things you did to me over the years. You made me do it! You made me sexually assault Dolly Lee! You did!"

He didn't put the knife down. He was seeking revenge. He knew he was going to get it one way or another. He was sure of it.

"No more, Mother! No more!"

A minute later, Lana screamed. The neighbors heard. It was her last.

Rubin had finally done it.

* * * * *

Rubin was put in handcuffs and led to a police car. He did not resist arrest. He didn't cry or say anything but, "I did it. I finally did what I had to do. It's all over now."

He said it quietly to the police, and to Mr. Colby, who stood as a witness for Rubin.

He confirmed Rubin's story. It was agreed that Lana was a sick woman, and that she made Rubin sick as well. He also told him about Dolly Lee who was now in an institution in Jackson, completely without speech. All this had made Rubin the way he was, and would be—for how long, no one knew.

Rubin did and said nothing during the trial. He sat with his head down in a daze, feeling doomed for life. He didn't care if he lived or died and he hated everything and everyone. His life was over. It had never even begun. Rubin had never been like other people, and never would be.

It was all Lana's fault. Though he killed her, her ghost would always be present in his mind. She would be with him forever—until he died. Only when he died would he finally be free of his mother. Death was his only alternative.

"We're putting you in Linwood, Mr. Clemmens," the judge stated. "It's a home for troubled youths like yourself. The doctors there will try to help you all they can."

There! The decision had been made! He was being put away. The judge never considered the fact that his dead mother would always be with him in spirit and would torment him to no end, just like when she was alive.

His life had ended—mentally. He'd never amount to anything now. He would be a brilliant young boy locked away from love and beauty—things the world had never offered him.

Mr. Colby tried consoling him. He patted him on the shoulder and gave him a piece of paper. "I'm still your friend, Rubin, so I'm giving you this. These are my office and home phone numbers. If you ever want to talk, just call. I'll always be here to help in any way I can.

"Also, I want you to know you're not a bad, worthless person because of what you've done. I don't feel or think you are. You're a troubled man who needs a friend, and that's where I come in. I want to help, and I will, if you let me."

A police officer announced, "Come on, Mr. Clemmens. It's time to go now."

Rubin said nothing. He just stared ahead as the police officer put him in the car and took him away to his new home—Linwood.

Mr. Colby stood watching. It was pathetic, a boy like Rubin. Life was cruel—so unfair, he thought.

He watched Rubin being taken away, feeling powerless and helpless.

Only fifteen years old, he mused. Fifteen years old and his life was over. No one cared. No one had done anything to help. It was the end.

PART THREE

ARLENE AND RUBIN THE BEGINNING

CHAPTER TWELVE

Linwood School for the Emotionally Disturbed was not as bad as one might think. The doctors and nurses made it their business to help each patient. Everyone there was to see that the patients ate, bathed, dressed, and had regular therapy sessions with a committed, qualified doctor.

Classes were held in regular subjects for the patients who were well enough to attend. Job assessment skills and placement services were also available when a patient was ready. They had entertainment, such as socials, parties, and dances. Birthdays and holidays were celebrated.

The patients ranged from thirteen to twenty-one years of age. If they didn't make substantial progress after their twenty-first birthday, they were sent to a different restricted environment.

Most of the patients had visitors and went home on holidays and weekends to be with their families and friends.

Arlene and Rubin had no one. As far as they knew, the school was their only home. They had their own private rooms. No one was allowed in anyone else's room without permission.

This was what Rubin wanted, to be alone like he had been all his life. He attended classes and studied in his room. He refused to go to the music room or to the gym and refused to participate in any sports. He bothered with no one, and just sat quietly in the doctor's office during his therapy sessions. He acknowledged no one and nothing. He was again alone, but this time by choice.

Arlene was alone, too. She had let herself go. Her beautiful blonde hair was matted. She refused to wash it. She seldom allowed herself to be cleaned. She wore the same short, matronly striped dress with a bulky sweater and no stockings, only scuffed shoes. Sometimes, though, she changed her clothes after urging by the aides.

Her eyes were often red, her face stained with tears. The people there tried to console her, but she rebuffed them.

She did attend classes, however, and did well, but the others in the class found her body odor repulsive, so she sat far away from everyone. She never participated in recreational activities.

They were two unhappy, lost souls locked away from the world. No one could reach them.

Arlene sat around in the halls, hunched forward, tears falling for hours. Her doctor tried talking with her, but she never responded to questions. She sat like a statue.

The doctor would put her arm around her, stroke her hair, and pat her hand, but she did not react to kindness. Dr. Reimes tried relentlessly, telling her that she was her friend and wanted to help her, but again—nothing.

"You're such a pretty girl, Arlene," Dr. Reimes said to her, holding her hand. "Why don't you go wash your face? You'd be much prettier if you did so. You have such lovely eyes, but they're always in tears. What's wrong? Why won't you relate to me?"

She'd go on relentlessly, never giving up or losing patience. After every session with Arlene, Dr. Reimes would be in tears, staring at her, watching her suffer, feeling powerless and helpless, unable to reach this tormented girl.

She knew of her past—about Charles Durning, her mother's husband. She knew of these things from Mrs. Greenworth and the police, who admitted Arlene to Linwood.

Dr. Reimes was perturbed by Arlene's case history of sexual abuse. She herself had been abused by her uncle, thus she knew how Arlene felt. That was why she had been assigned to be Arlene's therapist. She, too, became rebellious and headstrong, hating her uncaring, unbelieving mother. She knew and understood. Dr. Reimes, too, felt she hated men—all men—and would never let a man touch her, ever. She felt she had a chance to reach Arlene, to help her come to terms with her problems, thus she identified with Arlene being she, too, had suffered, but through therapy, the doctor had overcome her problems.

Dr. Johnson, Rubin's therapist, specialized in sexual problems of young boys. He helped young men deal with their sexual awareness. He dealt with rapists, molesters, voyeurs, and exhibitionists.

When he was a boy, he had a friend at school whose stepmother would approach the boy and try to seduce him. He had threatened her with a knife. She put him away.

This boy and he were close, though their backgrounds were different. Dr. Johnson's parents got along, worked, and were happy. This boy's father cared only for himself after his first wife, the boy's mother, died. He paid no attention to his second wife. Thus, she was like Rubin's mother, trying to turn him into her young lover.

Dr. Johnson had always wondered about him—his life now. He was probably dead now or suffering in some mental institution.

"I understand you," he told Rubin often. "I really do, and I can help you, but you won't let me. Why?" he asked continually.

Rubin sat staring ahead, not responding or reacting in any way.

"I know about you. Like Mr. Colby, I'd like to be a friend. He told me you were the smartest boy in school. I wasn't lucky enough to have your brains. You're a smart boy and can do anything you want—anything."

"Anything but make friends and have a girlfriend," Rubin said under his breath. "Thanks to Lana."

"What did you say, Rubin?"

"Nothing," Rubin replied without looking up.

"I heard what you said. Why don't you talk about your mother?"

"I have to go now," Rubin got up, not looking at him. "I have some studying to do."

"Good-bye, Rubin. The next time we'll talk more." Rubin left, saying nothing.

When he was in the hall, Rubin saw Arlene watching him, her hands on the railing of the stairs. He looked at her for a minute, picturing Dolly Lee and hearing voices—jeering voices from his past. He turned from her, walking on. She just stood and stared.

Carlos, another patient, went up to him and smiled. "Looks like she likes you, Rubie, baby."

Rubin ignored him but went on.

"Rubie, why don't you get it on?"

Rubin finally said, "Why don't you just piss off, you stupid jackass? You're really mental, you know that? A real sicko."

Carlos laughed. "You're the one who's crazy, with a crazy mother, liking male teachers, and sexually assaulting young girls. Why, everyone in this place knows about you."

The other patients started gathering in the hall, listening.

Carlos turned to them and pointed at Rubin. "Look at the weirdo, everyone! Here's a real one!"

Then to Arlene, he said, "Look at her!" He laughed aloud. "She sleeps with her stepfather, the pervert. Her old lady is a bitch in heat! Ha! Ha!"

Everyone stood watching.

Carlos didn't stop and laughed hysterically.

Rubin couldn't hold it in any longer. He jumped on him. Both were punching, kicking, and hitting, one on top of the other. Everyone was jeering. "Fight! Fight!"

Two attendants came and broke up the fight, each grabbing a boy and pulling them away from each other.

"All right now, both of you. Your doctors will hear of this in the morning. Now go back to your rooms, and not another word out of either of you. Understand?"

They turned to the others, "All right, everyone, go about your business, all of you."

"Arlene!" called a nurse from upstairs. "Come along now."

She did not answer. The nurse came down and gently led her up the stairs.

"Come on, honey. It's time for dinner."

Rubin thought of Arlene that night. Just like with Dolly Lee. Arlene liked him. She watched him. He looked at her, but of course he could never relate to her or any girl. He knew this, or so he thought.

This went on for a year—just watching and no verbal communication. That was it. No one knew. No one. There was nothing to know, it seemed. Nothing at all—unless Carlos said anything. However, it seemed no one cared.

CHAPTER THIRTEEN

Rubin was studying in the dayroom. He was surrounded by books on physics, chemistry, computers, and calculus. He copied ideas from one book, then another and another—absorbed in his books.

Arlene stood in the doorway, still dirty and disheveled, her large eyes watching him. Quietly, she walked toward the table, pulled up a chair, and sat down.

Rubin looked up at her, saying nothing. He looked at her and she him for a few minutes.

Finally, she took some paper and a pencil and wrote 'Hello' in big letters.

"Hello," he greeted quietly and politely.

She became perturbed. Her eyes looked angry. She wanted him to say more, but he didn't.

"What do you want?" he asked gently.

She just watched him. He said nothing.

Angrily, she ripped up the paper, threw it on the floor, then abruptly got out of her seat and turned away from him.

"Don't go," he said earnestly.

She turned to him, then she rushed out, with Rubin still watching the pained look on her face.

Arlene was in the hall, crying mutely with her hand resting on her arm on the wall. Carlos watched with a wicked smile on his face.

"You crybaby psycho, you!" he mocked.

"Leave her alone!" a voice called. "Just leave her be!"

Carlos turned and saw Rubin.

Carlos exclaimed, "Lover boy faggot!"

"Just leave her alone," Rubin stated again.

"Why? Do you like her or something?"

"Just let her be!"

"Make me, pervert!"

Rubin walked over and tried to grab Carlos by his shirt. He got scared and backed off.

* * * * *

"I see you made a friend," Dr. Johnson told Rubin at a session. "Arlene Gilbert. I saw you talking with her a couple of times."

Rubin's face clouded. He was indignant and said nothing.

"It's a good sign, you know." There was a pause. Neither said a word for a while.

"She isn't a friend."

Dr. Johnson said, "Don't be upset, Rubin. It's a positive sign—communicating with someone else. Interacting and caring are very important."

Rubin was still angry and said nothing.

The doctor was undaunted by his indignance, still trying to convince him he was showing improvement, and remained calm. Rubin was angry, and the doctor understood his anger. All his life he could never give or receive love appropriately.

Talking with Arlene was a good sign, but it didn't make Rubin feel better. He still thought of Dolly Lee. Look at what had happened. He had loved her, but he had sexually assaulted and hurt her. It was his fault. No—it was Lana's. Yes—Lana's. Lana's.

"Thank you, Mother," Rubin whispered angrily to himself.

"You're still upset with your mother, aren't you?"

Rubin didn't respond. Furiously, he jumped up and ran out the door.

Dr. Johnson called out, "Rubin!"

He ran off, not answering.

Arlene stood near the stairs, watching. Dr. Johnson saw her and said, "Hello." She said nothing. She just stared at him with deep fury.

Dr. Johnson smiled at her, but she left for the dayroom where she knew Rubin always went. He'd be there studying.

Arlene saw him reading his books. She walked over and sat down. He looked up.

"Go away, I'm busy," he said abruptly.

She put her hand on his arm, but he angrily jerked away.

"Go away! Get out of here!" he yelled at her.

She sobbed hysterically inside herself and pushed his books out of his hands, then roughly threw all the chairs on the floor.

Rubin got up. "Oh, God," he murmured. Then, to Arlene, he said, "Arlene, I-I—" he couldn't go on.

She stopped crying and stared at him with angry eyes.

"I'm sorry, Arlene. All right?"

She left the room, and he watched her go.

The two continued this relationship, weird as it was. Arlene would look at him, and he would talk to her. She would listen but say nothing. She began writing to him.

One day she wrote, 'Do you like me?'

Rubin was nonplussed. What a stupid question. Like her? Ridiculous! It was asinine. He didn't respond to her questions and continued studying. She just sat there, waiting.

'I like you,' she wrote on another piece of paper at last.

"Look, Arlene," he finally said, "I have a lot of studying to do. So, please, leave me alone!"

Tears came to her eyes. Angry, she ripped the pages up and threw them down.

"Oh, Jesus Christ!" he swore. "Not that again."

She sobbed and ran out the door.

She and Dr. Reimes continued their sessions. Arlene began writing her letters. She was starting to relate. First she was writing to Rubin, and now to her doctor.

In her English class, she was taught writing through various assignments. She had always been good in English. It was her favorite subject.

"Why don't you write a story about someone you love, Arlene?" the doctor suggested gently.

Arlene crossed her eyes angrily at Dr. Reimes, who persisted. "It'll be good for you. Please, Arlene, try. Try for me, okay?"

Arlene got up and left.

Outside the office, Arlene saw April, a snobbish girl from her English class.

"You really like Rubin, don't you? Well, honey," April said sarcastically, "he's mine. Do you hear me?"

"Leave her alone, April," an aide called out.

April ignored her and jeered at Arlene. "I'm prettier than you'll ever be, dearie. Rubin likes me. He told me so. You ask him," she went on, with Arlene not responding. "You're so ugly, no one would even look at you."

"April, that's enough," the aide retorted. "Now, you leave her be." She walked over, "Go on, now. Go!" She pushed her away from Arlene.

"Stupid bitch!" April cried out bitterly.

April Kincaid, at sixteen years, was the prettiest girl in the school. She had yellow hair, carefully curled, and had large, baby blue eyes. Her dresses were covered with bright floral prints.

Her parents were wealthy and owned a large merchandising business in town. She was committed because of her promiscuous behavior. She'd sleep with two or three boys a night in her parents' house and even tried to seduce her own father by standing nude in front of him.

She wasn't liked at the school, but she didn't care. She was pretty and wealthy—that's all that mattered, she felt.

April liked Rubin, but he ignored her. She pretended it wasn't so, and that he was just shy. He may have been, but he liked Arlene. April refused to believe this, and thus she tormented Arlene, made her cry, then April laughed hysterically.

"Hi, Rubin," she said sweetly, walking over to him like a model, dressed in a tube top that showed her breasts and a mini skirt just barely covering her. Her hair was put up.

Everyone watched her ogling Rubin. They laughed and called her a tramp. She gave them the finger and smiled wickedly.

"Up yours!" she said snottily.

Arlene watched and smiled. It was a real smile—her first in a very long time. She giggled to herself.

April was indignant when she saw Arlene laugh at her.

"What are you laughing about, you stupid bitch?" she snapped.

Arlene continued smiling, ignoring April's remark.

"Stop laughing, you bitch!" April screamed.

"Leave her alone, April, you mental moron, you!" another patient ordered.

"Make me! Just go ahead and try to make me!" April retorted.

"All right," an aide stated in a demanding voice from the far side of the room. "That's enough now! April, you go to your room. You've said enough!"

"No!" April yelled at the aide. The aide went over to her and took her wrist and led her out.

"Let go, you bitch! Let go!" She tried to jerk away.

The aide paid her no heed as they headed up the stairs.

"You bitch!" she said, sobbing, "You bitch!" she cried over and over.

Arlene stood smiling, watching the whole scene.

Rubin got up and walked over to Arlene and said, "Don't listen to her. She's an idiot."

Arlene smiled at him and put her hand on his shoulder. He didn't rebuff her.

"Let's go to the dayroom, okay?"

They went.

* * * * *

'I love you!' she wrote to Rubin constantly when they were alone in the dayroom.

He never responded, but would smile slightly more each time, and she always smiled back at him.

Arlene also took Dr. Reimes' suggestion and wrote about someone she loved. She had to do an assignment for her English class anyway, so why not use her therapist's idea for a class project?

Arlene worked diligently on it for a week. She wrote about Rubin. She liked him. She hardly saw him that week because she was so busy working on the project.

Dr. Reimes noticed the improvement in Arlene, although she still couldn't talk. Arlene began washing her face, and her hair once again became a deep yellow with her curls flowing. She wore a different dress each day—floral prints with pastel colors.

* * * * *

It had been over two years. Arlene was fifteen-and-a-half. She was now happy and her eyes were no longer filled with tears. She smiled more—at Rubin, at her doctor, and even at some of the other patients. She was completely undaunted by April's snotty remarks. She even laughed when April got teased about her promiscuity and attempts to get Rubin interested in her.

One day, April walked into the dayroom and saw Rubin. She smiled affectionately, gently massaging his shoulders. He jerked away and said, "Look, April, I'm not interested. Please go away. I'm busy."

"Oh, come on, Rubie, baby! You love it, you know you do!"

Rubin got indignant, "Look, please leave. I'm trying to do my work."

April said, "Why you little bum, you. You like that dirty, ugly bitch, don't you?"

Angry at that, Rubin got up and pushed April, pinning her against the wall.

"Don't you ever talk about Arlene like that, understand? Now go!"

She looked at him remorsefully with tears in her eyes.

"You'll be sorry. You will. You just wait and see!" she cried out.

As she left, Arlene walked in and smiled at Rubin. He smiled back, and she patted his hand as they sat.

'I love you!!' she wrote. 'I wrote about you for our English class.'

"Really? Why? Why me?" He was surprised.

Arlene shrugged, smiling. He returned her smile. She watched him for the rest of the afternoon.

CHAPTER FOURTEEN

April went into Arlene's room one night that week, smiling in a friendly manner.

When Arlene saw her, a perturbed look crossed her face. She didn't return her smile.

"Don't worry," said April, "I won't tease you, honest. You like Rubin, don't you? Oh, I forgot, you can't speak—but you can write, can't you? I'm not ridiculing you."

April saw the assignment on her desk, picked it up, and began to read. Arlene tried to stop her, but she was persistent. She kept reading.

"Good . . . good," she remarked as she read on. "This is really good, Arlene. I think it should be read to the class."

Arlene just stared blankly at her.

"I really think it's good. It should be read aloud. I'll read it for you. It shows promise. You can really write. I wish I could write like you. You're really smart. You get good grades. I wish I were as smart as you."

She stopped. Arlene just stared at her.

"I'll tell you what. I'll show you my room with all my clothes and things if you agree to let me read this, ok?"

Arlene took a piece of paper and wrote, 'Yes.'

April smiled, her eyes gleaming. Arlene had communicated to her. They left together.

* * * * *

Mrs. Greene began with the English assignment due that day. She asked if anyone wanted to have his or her report read aloud. April's hand was the first one to go up.

"All right, April," she smiled. "Why don't you begin?"

She smiled sweetly. "Oh, Mrs. Greene, it's not mine I wish to read. It's Arlene's. She said it was all right. Really, I think it's quite good."

"All right, April," she agreed. April got out of her seat and walked toward the front of the room with her head up high, smiling at Arlene.

She began: "Rubin—" Everyone turned toward him. He smiled back at them.

"How I love him so. I wish to make love to him like I did my Daddy Charlie Boy."

Everyone laughed. Mrs. Greene said angrily, "April!"

"Oh, how I'd like to touch him like he does me. Ah, his and mine together. I'm better than my mother."

Mrs. Greene rushed over and grabbed the paper from April's hand. "I said that's enough. You're in trouble, young lady!"

Arlene was shocked. She should have known. She got out of her seat and dashed out the door.

"Arlene!" Mrs. Greene called.

Everyone stared at Rubin. He blushed, ashamed. He felt as if he could never love anyone again.

* * * * *

That night, things changed. Rubin was in the study room with his books and Arlene walked in. She wanted to explain, but she couldn't. April had played a dirty trick on her, but she was unable to tell him about it.

He looked up, saw her, and said nothing. She wasn't writing, either. They both looked at each other for a few minutes with blank expressions on their faces.

Tormented, he couldn't contain himself any longer. He jumped out of his seat and pushed his books off the desk, then he went over to Arlene and pushed her off her chair. She fell to the floor. He slapped her and kicked her between her legs.

"Bitch!" he yelled repeatedly, still hitting her, pushing her, and kicking her with his foot.

Finally, he unzipped his pants, pulled them down, put his hand under her dress, pulled her panties down, and began to get an erection.

Arlene screamed silently, inside herself.

Rubin stopped himself, hanging his head in shame. "Oh, God!" he sobbed.

Quickly, Arlene got up and ran out the door, out of the school, and into the street blindly, not knowing what to do. Tears streamed down her face. Everyone in the street watched.

* * * * *

"Where is she?" Dr. Reimes asked Dr. Johnson as they sat in the lounge drinking tea.

No one knew.

It was late, and time for bed. No one could sleep. Everyone was upset. April was indignant. She wanted to go to bed.

"It's your fault," one patient said to her.

"Yeah!" another patient chimed in.

"All right, you two," an aide stated firmly. Then to April, she said, "I think you've been punished enough."

"It was my fault!" a voice called from the door. Everyone turned. It was Rubin.

"I hurt her. I hurt her bad," he announced flatly. "I suggest we call the police."

They did.

* * * * *

Arlene was still out in the street, lost. She looked around. People stared. She was drenched, tired, and hurting all over.

A police officer spotted her.

"Miss," he said gently, "Can I help you?"

Seeing she did not answer, he persisted. "Come with me!" He led her by the arm, but she jerked away.

"Please, miss, don't be afraid." He led her to his police car. "We'll help you."

Dejectedly, she went with him.

When they got to the precinct, the police officer saw another officer talking on the telephone.

"We'll try to find her, Doctor," he stated, then he hung up.

"Who was that?"

"A Dr. Reimes from the school. They called about a runaway mute girl," he replied.

At this, Arlene was led forward. "Sergeant, I found this girl alone in the street," the police officer announced.

He then glanced at her. "Why, that's the girl the school called about. Short, slim, blonde-haired person with brown eyes. Has she said anything?"

"No."

"That's her, definitely. She can't speak. That's what they told us. I tell you what . . . have her sit in the other room and I'll call the school to say we've found her."

"Fine," the police officer stated as he led Arlene into the next room.

* * * * *

"They've found her," Dr. Reimes announced to the others. To Dr. Johnson, she asked, "Do you want to come?"

Before he answered, Rubin piped up.

"Since it was my fault, I'd like to go along. I hurt her. I didn't mean to, as I said. Please," he implored.

The doctors looked at each other without saying anything for a while.

"All right, Rubin," Dr. Johnson replied. "Let's go."

* * * * *

The three drove downtown to the police precinct. Rubin wanted to be with Arlene alone. He told the doctors this, and they consented.

"She's in there," the sergeant said, pointing. The three stood. Rubin walked over to Arlene, shutting the door behind him. Arlene was hunched over, wrapping her sweater around her, her tear-stained face buried in her arms.

"Arlene," he said as he sat down beside her.

He said her name gently and raised his hand wanting to touch her, but he didn't dare to.

Slowly, she lifted her head and turned toward him, dry-eyed.

"You hurt me bad," she said softly and slowly.

"I'm sorry."

Then, he said with great excitement in his voice, "Arlene, you spoke! You can talk! Oh, Arlene!" he cried.

She smiled softly. "I love you."

He had tears in his eyes and was still smiling. "Oh, Arlene, I love you so. I'm so sorry for what happened."

They stood up and Rubin put his arms around her.

She hugged him, then they kissed. They liked it. They knew they loved each other.

"Let's go now," Arlene said quietly.

"Take my hand," Rubin said.

Slowly, their hands clasped. They walked out the door, smiling at each other.

PART FOUR
ARLENE AND RUBIN LATER

CHAPTER FIFTEEN

Arlene and Rubin were an item in the school now. In their English class, Rubin wrote, 'Rubin loves Arlene' surrounded by a heart on the blackboard. He told everyone that he loved her.

Arlene got up, faced the class, and smiled. All was well. April was furious, but who cared? Everyone laughed when she threw a tantrum, screaming and yelling and pounding her fists on the wall.

Mrs. Greene then spoke sharply "All right, class. Leave her alone. She was punished enough. Let her think about the commotion she caused, then perhaps she'll think about the consequences of her actions and learn appropriate behavior. Your laughter is uncalled for. She needs a lot of help."

The teacher stopped speaking, watching her class come to order. They were silent. Mrs. Greene resumed the lesson for that day.

* * * * *

They were always together. Arlene was sixteen and Rubin was eighteen. The improvement was there for everyone to see. Arlene wore her hair up and applied make-up. Rubin dressed up in a suit with a tie, his thick hair perfectly combed.

They had special privileges. They were allowed to go for walks together on the grounds. They received permission to go travelling into town together to shops, the local museum, and the park.

However, there was one problem that concerned both Dr. Johnson and Dr. Reimes—their parents. Rubin avoided talking about his mother. His doctor felt he needed to get into contact with his feelings to be able to deal with them appropriately.

The same was said of Arlene, whose mother was going to be discharged from Beekman and begin a new job working as a real estate agent in the city. The doctors thought of discussing their patients' case histories with each other.

Arlene and Rubin told each other about their parents.

"I hate her," Arlene said angrily.

"I understand," Rubin remarked. "My mother was no prize either."

"What do you mean?" she asked.

"She forced me to play sickly sexual games with her."

Arlene was horrified. Still, she felt he should talk about it.

He refused, and she didn't pursue the subject. Neither discussed it for the rest of the day.

It was a long while before the subject was brought up again.

* * * * *

"Why won't you talk about your mother?" Dr. Johnson asked him repeatedly, session after session.

Rubin would get angry and indignant.

Dr. Johnson continued. "You've improved a lot, Rubin. You not only found a friend, but a girlfriend who really cares about you. You know that. You didn't hurt Arlene—you've helped her by being her friend—but still it would be good if you talked more of your mother. Why do you supposed she treated you the way she did?"

Rubin shrugged.

"People act a certain way for a reason. It's true. No one just does things. Everything has a reason."

Rubin listened but said nothing.

"Do you remember your father?"

He shrugged, mumbling under his breath.

"I must go now. Arlene's waiting for me."

"Think about that last question, all right?"

Again, he shrugged, saying nothing as he went out the door.

* * * * *

"Think carefully, Rubin, about your father," Arlene said. "You told me he died when you were three, right?"

He nodded.

"Did your mother ever speak of him? Try to think before saying anything," Arlene went on.

"I guess so." He paused. "I suspect she was pregnant with me, and that's why they got married. She'd say that I was like him. She didn't mean it as a compliment, that's for sure," he said bitterly.

Arlene did not continue, but she felt she had made some progress with him. However, she still hated Juliajo—she thought. Juliajo had made her a mute for two years, and all because of Charles Durning—her wonderful knight in shining armor who threw them both into the street with no home, no money, and no friends.

Alone and defenseless, they had nowhere to turn. Arlene remembered it clearly—the hotel room and the beating from the woman who said she loved Arlene more than anything. She couldn't understand it. She wanted to believe her mother loved her, but if her mother loved her, why did she do what she did?

She worried relentlessly. It wasn't right, and she knew it.

* * * * *

"Dear sweet Lana," Rubin thought that night. "You're lucky I didn't hurt Arlene like I did Dolly Lee. You may be dead, Mother, but what you did will remain in my mind forever, though I love Arlene more than anything. She's a wonderful girl."

He continued thinking quietly into the night.

"Arlene is right. My mother was sick."

He thought of his father and tried to remember him. Finally, he fell asleep.

Later that night, when everyone was asleep, Rubin awoke with a scream of terror. Everyone got out of bed, questioning each other. What was that?

He screamed again.

Arlene knew it was Rubin. She ran from her room to Rubin, who was beating his head with his fists.

"Rubin, no!" she yelled, running toward him, holding him near her, stroking his back gently.

"It's all right," Arlene said, comforting him. "It's me—Arlene. It's all right."

"He hurt me!" he cried over and over.

No one else knew what he was talking about, but Arlene did.

"It's all right, darling," Arlene said again. "Please, Rubin, talk to me."

They continued holding each other.

Arlene looked up at the others. "It's all right, everyone."

Dr. Johnson walked in and saw Rubin.

"Are you ok, Rubin?"

Arlene answered, "Yes, Dr. Johnson. He's going to be ok," she assured him.

Dr. Johnson, Rubin, and Arlene were in his office the next day, discussing the night before.

"He remembers his father clearly now," Arlene gloated. "Oh, Rubin, I'm so happy. Now you can bury Lana. You now know why she was the way she was. You see, she needed love—a man's love, since she was rejected by your father. You were that man. Do you understand?"

Rubin nodded.

"She needed you in an unnatural sense," Dr. Johnson said.

"It's over now, Rubin," said Arlene. "Subconsciously you remembered your father through your dream of his cruelty toward your mother. It's too late for your mother, but not for you. You're going to be ok." She patted his hand and he squeezed hers. He was fine now.

CHAPTER SIXTEEN

A year later, Dr. Reimes announced to Arlene at a session, "Your mother called last night. She wants to see you."

Arlene was aghast.

She became angry and said nothing for a few minutes.

"I hate her!" she cried out passionately.

"I know you feel that way. Your mother made a lot of bad choices. Unfortunately, you were the one who suffered a lot of pain from her actions. But she now realizes how badly she hurt you. Just hear her out, for she is very bitter and remorseful and is deeply ashamed of her cruel treatment of you. She hates herself for it. And I do feel you think you hate her, but deep down you do not, you hate how she abused you. When you love someone and they do something wrong, you do not hate the person, you just think you do. For if you did, nothing would have been influential. Being hurt and angry may feel like hatred, but that is not true, and the hurt and anger may feel like hate, but are misunderstood and are two different issues."

She stopped to catch her breath, and then resumed, "But Arlene, you must understand, your mother was very troubled for a long time. She loves you."

"No, she doesn't," Arlene said repeatedly. "She made me sick for two years—two years!"

"Arlene," Dr. Reimes said gently, patting her hand. Arlene snatched her hand away, then got up quickly and turned to the wall.

"Arlene, your mother was sick all these years. She's just starting to get her life back together. She has her own apartment and a real estate job now. She'll need you."

"No!" shouted Arlene. "She let him sexually assault me. She didn't believe me. She hates me!" She was crying now, ignoring what Dr. Reimes told her.

But she was not deterred. She understood but tried to get Arlene to understand her mother's turmoil and behavior toward her, insisting she loved her and deserved another chance.

"Arlene, please believe me, she does love you. Why won't you see her? You need to. You must."

Arlene ran out of the office. Rubin saw her, took her arm, and said, "Arlene?" She didn't answer him but kept on running.

"Arlene, what's wrong?" Rubin called after her. There was still no reply.

She avoided him for the rest of the day.

* * * * *

"Why didn't you talk to me yesterday?" Rubin asked Arlene the next day.

"My mother wants to see me."

They stood there and said nothing for a while.

"You know I hate her. You know that!"

"No, you don't. You don't, and you know it. You're upset with her and hurt but think of what she's been through. She's hurting, too. She went through a lot—first your father, then her husband."

"She tried to kill me that night in the hotel, did you forget that?"

"No, I didn't, but from what I heard, she loves you. Please, Arlene."

She stared at him for a while. There was a long, loaded pause. Then she walked away and spoke to no one for the rest of the day.

* * * * *

A week later, Dr. Reimes told Arlene her mother was waiting to see her in the visitor's lounge.

Arlene didn't want to see her. She could not. It was as simple as that. Her mother was dead to her and always would be. She hated her and wanted no part of her—ever.

However, through Dr. Reimes' persuading, she grudgingly went to the lounge.

Juliajo was standing facing the window opposite the door. Arlene saw her, then Juliajo turned and saw her as well. Neither said anything for a while.

Juliajo was definitely older, but still not bad looking. She still had sparkling eyes made-up, and her hair was still blonde, a little less than shoulder length.

"Arlene," she said quietly.

Arlene didn't return the greeting. Her eyes were angry. The hurt was still there.

"Oh, Arlene!" she cried out, running toward her with her arms opened. "My darling little girl."

Arlene abruptly turned away from her.

"Arlene, please!" she sobbed. "I-I love you! I do. You must believe that!" The tears were streaming down her face, smearing her make-up. Arlene was watching her. She wanted to believe her. She did, in part, but part of her refused.

"Go away! I hate you!" she yelled at her mother.

"Arlene!" she said. "Please understand."

An aide then walked in. "I think you've had enough for today, Arlene, Ms. Gilbert."

"Please, let me stay just for a few more minutes."

"You may visit next week, according to her doctor's orders."

Juliajo left, dejectedly. 'Arlene will never forgive me,' she thought. 'She hates me. The hurt is still there.'

She told Dr. Reimes what happened. Dr. Reimes assured her that all that was needed was time and patience. Juliajo would have to hold out longer—how long, no one knew.

* * * * *

Arlene bothered with no one that whole week, not even Rubin, who became furious with her.

"Damn you, Arlene!" he shouted. "She's your mother. She loves you. Sure, she hurt you, but she's only human. Now today, when she comes, you're going to be nice and friendly and listen to her. She's your mother for Christ's sake—your mother. You got me to forgive my mother, now you do it!"

Arlene didn't argue with him. He was right and she knew that quite well. She was determined to see her mother. It would be hard for her, but she had to. It was only correct that she do so.

* * * * *

"Your mother is here, Arlene," called an aide.

Arlene got up. Rubin said, "Remember what I said, now. Be nice. Forgive and forget. She's your mother."

When Arlene entered the lounge, Juliajo was sitting near the window.

"I was young and naïve. I believed your father loved me. He didn't. I was alone. I met Charles. He was nice at the beginning. Suddenly it ended. It wasn't that I didn't believe you. I didn't want to. I believed Charles loved us. I mean, I worked for him, married him—and then it happened. He stopped caring." Her voice was rising. "I don't know what happened, honestly. I got confused and frustrated, but I never stopped loving you."

She stopped again, then with tears in her voice, she went on. "I took it out on you. I'm sorry." The tears poured out.

Arlene watched her—her mother. She loved her. She now knew she did. Juliajo turned from her daughter, staring out the window.

Arlene walked over to her and gently put her hand on her shoulder.

"Mama," she said quietly.

Her mother turned toward her and held her close. Arlene reciprocated.

"I love you, Mama."

"Oh, Arlene," Juliajo said breathlessly, still holding her.

Arlene kissed her on the cheek.

"It's been so long," Juliajo remarked. "We have so much to say. So much."

Arlene smiled. "Yes, Mama."

They clasped hands, smiling with tears in their eyes. They loved each other now, and always would.

CHAPTER SEVENTEEN

Rubin was graduating from his class in two months. Naturally, he did quite well. He would be receiving Honors at commencement exercises. He wanted to study engineering at college.

Dr. Johnson felt his progress was excellent. He talked now to the people in his class, to his doctor, and most importantly, to Arlene, whom he wanted to marry.

Arlene had one more year of schooling left before she graduated. She did, however, accept Rubin's proposal.

Much had to be considered before they could even contemplate marriage. Jobs? A home? Schooling? Both Dr. Johnson and Dr. Reimes had to collaborate with them to help them. True, they had improved, but that was in a hospital setting. What about life on the outside in the real world?

Rubin was to work as an electrical consultant part-time with a partial scholarship to Poly Tech. Arlene would tutor English part-time.

Where would they live? They didn't make much money to live even in a little apartment.

Much had to be decided before they married.

* * * * *

"Oh, Arlene," he addressed his beloved one day as they strolled in the park. "How I love you so."

He held her by the waist, and she did so with him as well. They gazed at each other, saying nothing.

He was dressed casually for a change. He wore jeans with a checkered shirt. She was wearing a yellow strapless tube top with blue shorts. For once, his hair was ruffled. Hers was put up in pins, disheveled.

They clasped hands and strolled to the lake, then Rubin said, "I'll race you."

Arlene laughed as she started to run, "Last one to the lake is a rotten egg!" she shouted.

Rubin giggled, chasing after her. When he finally caught her, he grabbed her, and they kissed.

"Oh, Rubin," she said playfully as they tumbled down on the grass. He pinned her to the ground and began tickling her. She laughed.

"Do you love me?" he asked.

"No," she replied, teasing him.

"No?" he questioned, knowing she was only teasing.

They kissed again, holding each other for a while.

They were happy. They loved each other. They meant the world to each other. They were with each other, and no one and nothing else mattered.

However, they had their futures to think of. They wanted to get married, have a home, jobs, children, and a life for themselves. They wanted to be free and enjoy their lives together. According to their therapists, much had to be considered first. Rubin and Arlene were at their mercy. Their lives depended upon others.

* * * * *

"Marriage is a big commitment," Dr. Reimes explained to Arlene and Rubin at a session with Dr. Johnson. "I know you love each other and want to be together, and that's good, but you're both very young and inexperienced. Marriage is not something to jump into."

"I want you two to be together. I want you to be happy and enjoy life, but you must consider a lot of things," Dr. Johnson stated.

To Arlene, he said, "You have one more year of schooling." To Rubin, he stated, "How would you support Arlene? You'll be too busy with your job and studies to devote yourself to marriage."

Then Dr. Reimes mentioned, "Arlene, your mother wants you to live with her. I think it's a promising idea. You'll attend classes in your hometown."

Arlene's eyes brightened, but before she said anything, the doctor went on. "I spoke with her a few times. We both think you're well enough to go live with her. She wants you to. As for you, Rubin, you're very much improved. You'll live at the dormitory of your college, as well as work at your job."

Dr. Johnson then chimed in. "Both of you have come a long way, and we want more than anything to see you happy and together, but you simply can't get married right away. You understand, don't you?"

Both nodded.

The decision was made. It made Arlene and Rubin a little perturbed, but they realized the obstacles involved in rushing into marriage. They understood.

Rubin would attend college and marry Arlene after he graduated and secured a steady, well-paying job as a research scientist.

Arlene would live at home, finish her schooling, graduate, and get a job tutoring English while attending college to study writing, since that was what she wanted to do for a living.

They were jubilant. They would be together always in body and soul, loving each other and making their own mature decisions. They agreed to write and call each other, and Rubin would come in and visit Arlene on holidays and during summer vacations. Love was challenging work. Much was to be sacrificed, but their love was a thing to be cherished forever.

* * * * *

It was June. Rubin's graduation was taking place. He was valedictorian of his class. Arlene came with her mother. They were all Rubin had in his life, but it was enough to let him know he was loved.

Rubin was handsome in his beige suit with a striped, brown tie. His thick jet-black hair shone, and he brushed and parted it on the side perfectly. Not a strand of hair was out of place.

Arlene's hair was done high in curls. She wore a pink floral halter dress, and her face was made up with powder, rouge, lipstick, and eye shadow.

Juliajo was proud. Rubin was like a son to her. She was happy Arlene had found a nice young man. She wanted the best for her daughter. She only prayed Rubin wouldn't turn out to be another Spencer or Charles.

"I love her, Ms. Gilbert, and you need not worry. Arlene is the only one for me and always will be," Rubin said, and he meant it.

After the ceremony, Rubin met up with Arlene and Juliajo. Arlene ran up, threw her arms around his neck, and kissed him.

"You were great, honey!" she exclaimed.

He pecked Juliajo on the cheek. She smiled, and then said, "Let's all go out for coffee."

"Yeah!" Arlene and Rubin agreed in unison.

EPILOGUE

Four years later, Rubin and Arlene got married and bought a small home in the suburbs. They went to Nashville for two weeks for their honeymoon. He works as a supervisor of Research Sciences for a metal firm. Arlene attends writing classes part-time at a local college and is doing well. She authors stories, poems, and articles for a small magazine in the town where she lives.

True, they have their problems and disagreements, but all has ended well for both. They want to take a trip to Europe. Both want a baby. They realize they can't have all the things they want right away. It will take time and patience, as well as money, but together they are able to make their way through for they love each other and do trivial things for each other to make their lives happy. He buys her presents and takes her on weekends upstate. She writes him love poems and cooks his favorite dishes.

Their pasts do not haunt them as they did years ago. Rubin has finally buried Lana for good. Arlene does not rehash or think about Charles, and has maintained her loving relationship with Juliajo, who has become quite successful at her job and in life.

RECOMMENDED RESOURCES

ORGANIZATIONS FOR CHILDREN WITH SPECIAL NEEDS

EASTER SEALS

233 South Wacker Drive, Suite 2400
Chicago, Illinois 60606
312-726-6200
800-221-6827

1841 State Route 35#B
South Amboy, New Jersey 08879
732-316-0906

1 Olive Street
Perth Amboy, New Jersey 08861
732-442-5745
Fax: 312-726-1494

25 Kennedy Blvd., Suite 600
East Brunswick, New Jersey 08816

141 Headley Terrace
Irvington, New Jersey 07111-1320
973-351-0172

141 West Jackson Blvd
Chicago, Illinois 60604
312-726-6200
800-221-6827

515 Valley Street, Suite 180
Maplewood, New Jersey 07040
973-313-0976

11 Freeman Street
West Orange, New Jersey 07052
973-677-7366

SPECIAL OLYMPICS

1133 19th Street NW
Washington, DC 20036-3604
1+202-628-3630 and 800-708-8585
Fax: 202-824-0200

THE ARC

1158 Wayside Road
Tinton Falls, New Jersey 07712
732-493-1919

FRIENDSHIP CIRCLE INTERNATIONAL

816 Eastern Parkway
Brooklyn, New York 11213
718-713-3062

GOODWILL INDUSTRIES INTERNATIONAL

25 Elm Plaza 3rd Floor
Brooklyn, New York 11201-5355
718-246-4905

PARENTS HELPING PARENTS

545 8th Avenue
New York, New York 10018
845-230-8045

FEDERATION FOR CHILDREN WITH SPECIAL NEEDS

529 Main Street, Suite 1M3
Boston, Massachusetts 02129
617-236-7210
800-331-0688

SPECIAL NEEDS ALLIANCE

7739 East Broadway Blvd, Suite 362
Tucson, Arizona 85710

FAMILY VOICES

110 Hartwell Avenue
Lexington, Massachusetts 02421
781-674-7224

ORGANIZATIONS FOR CHILD SEXUAL ABUSE

DARKNESS TO LIGHT

4900 O'Hear Avenue, Suite 205
North Charleston, South Carolina 29405
866-forlight or 843-965-5444

CHILD WELFARE INFORMATION GATEWAY

800 4.A. Child 800-422-4453

SAFE HORIZON

50 Court Street, 8th Floor
Brooklyn, New York 11201
347-328-8110

NATIONAL COALITION TO PREVENT CHILD SEXUAL ABUSE AND EXPLOITATION

National Runaway Safe Line
@1800 Runaway
Jacob Wetterling Resource Center
@jwrcsafekids

ORGANIZATIONS FOR CHILD ABUSE

BOYS TOWN

14100 Crawford Street
Boys Town, Nebraska 68610
531-355-1111

PREVENT CHILD ABUSE AMERICA

228 South Wabash Avenue, 10th Floor
Chicago, Illinois 60604
Email: info@preventchildabuse.org

SAFE HORIZON

30 Bay Street, Suite 506
Staten Island, New York 10301
718-720-2591
320 Schermerhorn Street
Brooklyn, New York 11217
718-330-5400

CHILDREN'S RIGHTS

88 Pine Street, Suite 800
New York, New York 10005
212-683-2210

ORGANIZATIONS FOR DOMESTIC VIOLENCE

NATIONAL COALITION AGAINST DOMESTIC VIOLENCE

1-800-799-7233(SAFE)

WOMEN RISING

270 Fairmount Avenue
Jersey City, New Jersey 07306
201-333-5700

NEW YORK CITY ANTI-VIOLENCE PROJECT

116 Nassau Street
New York, New York 10038
212-714-1186

SAFE HORIZON

2 Lafayette Street
New York, New York 10007
212-577-7780

WOMAN KIND

32 Broadway, 10th Floor
New York, New York 10004-1507
212-732-0054

BULLYING

OLWEUS BULLYING PREVENTION PROGRAM

321 Brackett Hall
Clemson, South Carolina 29634

NATIONAL BULLYING PREVENTION CENTER

80 E. Hillcrest Street, Suite 203
Thousand Oaks, California 91360
1-800-273-8255
Spanish Speakers: 1-888-628-9454
8161 Normandale Blvd.
Bloomington, Minnesota 55437

STAMP OUT BULLYING

877-NOBULLY
877-602-8559